RAZORBILL

(YOU) SET ME ON FIRE

Writer and performer MARIKO TAMAKI has garnered much acclaim for both her written and performance-based work. The graphic novel *Skim* (with Jillian Tamaki) was shortlisted for the Governor General's Award and received numerous other accolades, including the Doug Wright Award for Best Graphic Novel. You can follow Mariko on her blog at marikotamaki.blogspot.com and on Twitter at @marikotamaki.

D1602218

(you) set
me on fire

mariko tamaki

razOr
bill

RAZORBILL
an imprint of Penguin Canada

Published by the Penguin Group
Penguin Group (Canada), 90 Eglinton Avenue East, Suite 700, Toronto, Ontario, Canada
M4P 2Y3 (a division of Pearson Canada Inc.)

Penguin Group (USA) Inc., 375 Hudson Street, New York, New York 10014, U.S.A.
Penguin Books Ltd, 80 Strand, London WC2R 0RL, England
Penguin Ireland, 25 St Stephen's Green, Dublin 2, Ireland (a division of Penguin Books Ltd)
Penguin Group (Australia), 250 Camberwell Road, Camberwell, Victoria 3124, Australia
(a division of Pearson Australia Group Pty Ltd)
Penguin Books India Pvt Ltd, 11 Community Centre, Panchsheel Park, New Delhi – 110 017, India
Penguin Group (NZ), 67 Apollo Drive, Rosedale, Auckland 0632, New Zealand
(a division of Pearson New Zealand Ltd)
Penguin Books (South Africa) (Pty) Ltd, 24 Sturdee Avenue, Rosebank,
Johannesburg 2196, South Africa

Penguin Books Ltd, Registered Offices: 80 Strand, London WC2R 0RL, England

First published 2012

1 2 3 4 5 6 7 8 9 10 (WEB)

ONTARIO ARTS COUNCIL
CONSEIL DES ARTS DE L'ONTARIO

Lyrics from "Teenage Romanticide" by Dance Yourself to Death used with permission.

Manufactured in Canada.

LIBRARY AND ARCHIVES CANADA CATALOGUING IN PUBLICATION

Tamaki, Mariko
(You) set me on fire / Mariko Tamaki.

For ages 14+
ISBN 978-0-14-318093-7

I. Title. II. Title: You set me on fire.

PS8589.A768Y69 2012   jC813'.6   C2012-903188-7

Visit the Penguin Canada website at www.penguin.ca

Special and corporate bulk purchase rates available; please see
www.penguin.ca/corporatesales or call 1-800-810-3104, ext. 2477.

ALWAYS LEARNING   PEARSON

For Lindy Zucker. With two barrels.

I was a victim of teenage
romanticide, and in the wrong.

I was a victim of teenage
romanticide, but not for long.

~ Dance Yourself to Death

ONE

A brief but necessary descent into flames

This is a story about college, about fire, and also about love.

Before going to college at the age of seventeen, I'd been in love once (total catastrophe) and on fire twice (also pretty bad). In fact, I almost didn't get to go to college at all because I accidentally set myself on fire in an incident that was at least partly connected in some way to love.

When I say "accidentally," I mean that there was fire and there was me but the almost fatal combination of the two was not some sort of big master plan. It wasn't a suicide fire, if there is such a thing. It was more of a "whoops" fire, an "I can't believe I set myself on fire" kind of fire. A "holy shit" fire.

You get the picture.

Of course, what makes the whole thing kind of complicated to explain was the fact that when I accidentally set myself on fire a month before I was supposed to go to St. Joseph's College, it wasn't the first time I'd been on fire that year, or even that summer. Although, I should point out, the first time I was on fire, it wasn't really my fault.

If anyone was to blame for my first fire, it was this girl, Julia.

Julia was the only girl in my high school more unpopular than I was. I was the kind of person people avoided, I would guess, because I emanated waves of uncool. No matter what I did, I was uncool. It was an ugly sweater I could never get rid of. At some point I just took to wearing ugly sweaters and jeans. Why not embrace it? Better than looking like you're fighting for a hopeless cause. What is that saying, dressing up a pig? Or something.

I'm not saying I'm a pig, but you get the idea.

Julia was scary unpopular, the girl everyone avoided because she was clearly insane. One time in grade five she "carelessly but not necessarily purposefully" (according to our principal) broke Susan Levine's hand by stepping on it a number of times. In grade ten she *mistakenly* threw acid into Sarah Mather's knapsack in chemistry when she didn't get picked for the basketball team. The only reason why Julia wasn't kicked out of school was her billionaire grandfather, who invented diets for rich people.

After the acid thing, supposedly they put her on medication that made hurting other people less of a probability.

Technically, it was Julia who invited me to prom. She'd cornered me at my locker a week before what our school was calling "A Night of Magic" and announced, in a voice that was slightly unsteady, that her boyfriend had been arrested for assault and so she had two "Magic" tickets and a limo but no date.

How could I say no, especially with Julia huffing and puffing in an unnatural way an inch from my face?

I'm sure that any relief my parents felt when they heard I was going to prom was obliterated the minute Julia cruised up in her SUV limo, hanging out of the sunroof with a bottle of Diet Spritz that clearly wasn't Diet or Spritz and a face full of runny mascara, looking like a psychopathic jack-in-the-box on wheels.

At some point, possibly while I was taking the first of many slugs of Julia's non-pop in order to wash down a small yellow pill she'd handed me when I shuffled into the limo, Julia, who had apparently forgotten that SHE invited ME to prom, leaned over and mumbled, "If it sucks, I'm going to be mad."

"It won't suck," I said.

I won't go into the specifics, but of course it did blow, both in the way all proms suck because the reality of prom can never live up to the promise, and in the way proms suck when you don't have a posse and are instead the drunken member of an army of two.

By the end of the night, sitting in the backyard of Dawn Garner, class president, Julia was a stretch lace and velvet ball of mess.

"It's good we're getting out of here," she slurred. "All the people at this school are assholes."

True, I thought, silently chewing on the word with my brain because I was too drunk and drugged at the time to say anything out loud.

The incendiary part of this story happened shortly after that statement. Apparently, sometime around midnight, Susan—the same Susan whose hand Julia had mashed in grade five—came out into the backyard and called Julia something not very nice. Julia retaliated by throwing her beer and yelling something about Susan having herpes. Susan called Julia a "freak show" and then Julia stood up, held out her cigarette to me, and said, "Hold this."

Or "Take this."

Something.

Unfortunately, just as Julia was getting ready to kick ass, I was in the process of passing out, a course of action that involved me slowly checking out of my brain and body until all was black and quiet. So I wasn't paying all that much attention to what Julia was saying or what she was doing with her lit cigarette. How it came to be that Julia's cig ended up wedged into the pink plastic rose corsage pinned to my dress strap instead of between my index and middle finger, I do not know. It's possible that I wedged the cigarette in there myself, although I have no memory of doing this. What I do know is that, as Julia was curling her manicured hands around Susan's boyfriend's neck, I was smouldering. Literally. Thankfully, just as the plastic roses began melting into my neck, I woke up and, with a ninja-type grace, threw my Coke on myself before I dropped to the ground.

Someone, jumping the gun slightly, yelled, "Fire!"

The thing that occurred to me later, as I sat in the ER surrounded by an evening's worth of the broken, the bleeding, and the barfing, was how weird it is that people are apparently more likely to come running when someone yells "Fire" than when someone yells "Help" or "Rape."

I've always wanted to test that theory, but I figure the consequences for yelling "Help" or "Fire" if you don't need help and you're not on fire are pretty

5

major. I should try yelling "Help" the next time I'm on fire, I suppose. See if that makes a difference.

Although, you know, I was thinking about it and, okay, so doesn't this whole "Help" and "Fire" thing make women who need help and yell "Fire!" into liars?

I think that (also) kind of sucks.

I guess it suggests that sometimes there are good reasons for lying about these things.

Standing in front of my parents in the living room at three a.m., post-prom, I tried to be as vague as possible in describing the sequence of events that had led to a ponytail's worth of singed hair and a hornet's nest of nasty-looking blisters on my left shoulder. I focused on the fact that the paramedics who'd taken me to the hospital—largely, I insisted, out of precaution—had told me that prom was a particularly bad time to get set on fire because everyone wears really flammable stuff and then gets loaded. I asked one paramedic if this meant that lots of kids are set on fire at their proms.

"Nope," the guy taking my pulse said. "You're the first."

Apparently, the biggest injury that happens at prom is alcohol poisoning. No big surprise.

Twisting the handle on the bag that contained my singed prom dress and heels, I did my best to put a positive spin on the whole situation.

"Other than the really, really small fire," I gushed, "I had a really good time. Really. Great DJ."

My father, still in pyjamas and bathrobe, sighed heavily.

My mother stood and grabbed the aloe plant sitting on the windowsill. "Go get your pyjamas on and meet me in the kitchen," she said. "Let's see if we can at least avoid a scar."

The second time I was on fire was more what you'd actually call being on fire, flames instead of embers. It happened as I was in the process of burning some possessions, including some childhood relics and a select group of memories I'd held onto from a certain person. (Okay. Her name is Anne. I will talk about her later.) I figured that a fire would be more fun than just scooping everything up in a big garbage bag, so I constructed a funeral pyre in the backyard on the rock platform my dad had made for us to roast marshmallows over when I was a kid.

I was listening to "Forever Young" on my iPod and watching the sparks from my small collection of notes/letters, cradled in the arms of some old stuffed animals, climb into the night sky. Just as I started lip-synching the chorus I noticed a pool of

toxic chemicals, presumably the melting remains
of formerly happy plastic-animal faces, sliding off
the rock platform and into my mother's bed of
perennials. As I turned to kick dirt onto the sludge,
my cape caught fire.

I should add here that this was a magic cape my
mom made me years ago for a school play, and that I
was wearing it because it just happened to be packed
up with the stuffed animals. It's not like I'm the sort
of person who wears a cape on any regular basis.

So once again it was all stop, drop, and roll.

And this time it was my neighbours, who'd been
watching my antics while they sat and drank their
nightly sherry, who called 911.

After I'd managed to set myself on fire for a second
time, I think my parents were sincerely considering
locking me up in some sort of cage instead of
sending me off to college. I'm sure they were a bit
torn because, on the one hand, I had clearly become
the world's most troublesome daughter and they
were kind of happy about the idea of getting rid
of me and having the place to themselves. On the
other hand, their precarious love for me made them
worried, I think, that if they left me to my own
devices I would blow myself up.

It was about this time, I'm sure, that they started
seriously regretting their bright idea to fast-track me

into high school by skipping grade eight, a decision they'd made on the basis of a single (but apparently important) aptitude test I don't even remember taking. One test score earned at the age of eleven and I spent my early teen years being that little bit less mature than the people around me. Hard to say if that really matters. Aren't all teenagers immature?

My dad said he wanted to think on it before he'd agree to sign the parental-consent section of my St. Joseph's residence acceptance form. He thought about it for three days. I don't know what made up his mind, but on the day he told me he would sign the form, my dad gave me a big lecture about "decision-making" and me and what I'd been doing with my young life.

At the time, my skin was still sore to the touch. The blisters from my first burn had healed only to be eclipsed by a new rash of crispy soreness. The area around my shoulder and neck was a patchwork quilt of hard bits and baby skin. Parts of my body looked like something you'd find spinning behind the counter at a gyro restaurant.

"I just want you to think, Allison," he said, "about what it means that this has happened to you twice. Just think about it, okay?"

"Okay."

"I know you've had—" My father struggled at the

best of times with emotional topics. The only way he could talk to me about any of this stuff was to be doing some sort of physical labour in the process. For example:

Drugs → Fixing the Toilet

Pregnancy → Mowing the Lawn

(And you know, for that last one I could barely hear him, so for the longest time I thought I'd be going on some sort of "bill.")

He was washing the dishes when he approached the subject of me and my recent series of misfortunes. "I know you've had some trouble. I know there was that girl."

"Yeah."

"Annie?"

"No, but. It doesn't matter."

"I know she was important to you. And I'm sorry. I'm sorry you've had kind of a … a tough break with that."

"Right."

It's painful to see the effects of your messed-up-ness reflected in the eyes of the people you care about.

"You're a smart girl."

"Thanks."

"Maybe you could be a little bit ... smarter."

"Sure."

I remember looking at the sun hitting my dad's hands as he scratched little bits of food that looked like my scabs off a dinner plate.

"Get me that form for your residence and a pen."

And with that, I was officially off to St. Joseph's.

I know some people funnel a lot of their hopes and dreams into their college choice. I did too, but not in that cheesy, fairy tale, "I wanna go to Harvard so I can become president" way you see in movies. I picked St. Joseph's because, of the seven schools I applied to, it was as far away from my high school as I could manage on my (parents') budget. (I'd also applied, on a whim, to go to this school in France and one in Russia but I didn't get in, probably because I had such crappy marks in French and Russian.) Based on an informal poll, I'd calculated that it was also the only college no other people from my graduating class would be attending. No less than five states and two bodies of water separated it from most of the people I knew.

Driving to St. Joseph's, I took a closer look at my final acceptance papers and noticed that the college mascot, which I'd originally thought was an eagle (like every other college mascot), was a phoenix.

I've never actually read the myth of the phoenix. This may seem surprising, or maybe it's not, because no one reads anything anymore. I wouldn't even know where to start looking for it. I'm sure it isn't just in some book written by some guy. It's probably in a collection. To find that collection I'd probably have to know what KIND of myth it is. And I don't.

What I do know, I know from Harry Potter and Wikipedia. I know that the phoenix—I think it's a he—willingly enters the flames as a kind of ugly, weak, crispy old bird, and (maybe an hour) later, emerges from those flames vibrant and heroic, like something you'd expect to see in a commercial for something awesome.

I know that the phoenix is no masochist, no accident-prone bird, although possibly the other birds would argue otherwise. I don't picture the phoenix as being very social, more like the mad genius no one wants to eat lunch with. A non-social drinker.

A possible drug abuser.

I'm well acquainted with the perils of drugs because before we left, my dad got his sister, who's a nurse, to put together a bunch of pamphlets about drug abuse and alcohol poisoning. I was supposed to be reading these pamphlets on the trip (with the possibility of a pop quiz during the last twenty-mile leg)—a trip my mother declined to join because long roads (and my dad's driving habits on long roads) make her queasy. Hilariously, for some reason, the jog across the country reminded my dad of all his fun-filled college days. So for most of the ride I ended up listening to stories about what my dad's frat brothers got up to when he was at Michigan State U.

I'll spare you the details. Suffice to say, the majority of it was weird *American Pie*–type stuff that no daughter needs to hear about.

Wrapping up a story involving a sheep, a bicycle pump, and several buckets of Jell-O, my dad chuckled, "Do what I say not what I do, of course. Don't tell your mother I told you that story."

"I won't."

"I mean, you know, your dad was a crazy guy. And you, ah, need to be, you know. Just be careful out there. You got … you got … uh."

"I know, Dad."

The phoenix can dip into fire to transform himself whenever the moment strikes him, but humans, I knew, having been warned by several doctors, can only get rid of so many layers of skin.

FIRST TERM

Attention Dylan Hall Residents!!!!

Please Note: There are <u>no</u> flammable objects allowed in the dorm. These objects would include: incense, candles, scented candles, cigarettes, fireworks, and any other incendiary devices.

This is for YOUR SAFETY!

Any resident caught with any of the above objects will be subject to a fine.

TWO

Dis orientation
(is a huge waste of time)

The funny thing about going to college is that it's not some place you just GO. It's automatically a new start, which somehow automatically requires a massive group orientation—i.e.: freshman year and freshman orientation.

A couple words about orientation week: it sounds very serious and important, like something you cannot miss. Like, if you don't go, you won't be oriented. Like, this is where they give you your special college campus decoder iPhone app, compass, and "You Are Here" map.

The truth is, there's nothing less important in this world than orientation week. First of all, everything you need to know about any college is on its website. Orientation is just a bunch of get-to-know-you games and commercially sponsored events. Which, to ME, means you should be able to opt out. Like, no thanks, I'm good.

Right?

Wrong.

I was caught in its clutches the second my dad released me from a mammoth goodbye hug on the curb outside Dylan Hall, St. Joseph's only all-girls residence—a massive red-brick, silo-shaped column of a building just off the main road and two minutes from the main campus gates.

"Sure you don't want me to walk you in? Get you settled?" My dad smiled what seemed to be a bit of a nervous smile.

"No. I just. It's cool. It's a long drive back and ... Anyway. Thanks."

Still imprinted with the smell of my dad's aftershave, I stepped through Dylan's thick wooden front doors and into the white-on-white main hall of my new residence only to be confronted by a very tall woman with an intimidating southern belle–sized cloud of blond hair and a red and white U REP shirt.

"Hey!" she squealed, one arm up in a big wave, like I was someone she was meeting for coffee who was five minutes late. "Hey! I'm Joy! Welcome to Dylan Hall! How are you!?"

"Hey," I echoed back with significantly less enthusiasm. "Uh, this is my residence. I mean, uh, good, I think. I have my letter in my bag if ..."

"Well let's just get you your room number then," Joy trilled as she pulled out a red clipboard of residents and room numbers, flipped through a few pages, and bobbed her head from side to side a bit before giggling. "OH my goodness! I need your name first. HELLO, JOY! You are?"

"Uh. Allison. With two l's and an i. Lee, two e's."

"Yup, yup, yup, no, yup. Oh, HERE you are!" Joy looked up from her list to give me another smile, which shattered when her eyes hit the sore spots that ran from the hairline on the left side of my face down to and under the edge of my shirt. "Oh my goodness, AH-llison, what happened to your skin? Are you okay?"

"OH!" I sputtered, "Oh yeah. Um. Yeah. It's an old injury. Just. You know. Heh heh. He-healing." I was suddenly sweating like a can of soda on a sunny day. "You, uh, have a room number for me?" I inquired somewhat weakly. "Or, um ..."

"Oh right. Yeah." Reaching behind her, Joy grabbed a blue plastic bracelet, not unlike the ones they give you in the hospital, and quickly, with single-handed efficiency, clipped it around my wrist. "You're floor eleven, room seven. Right, that's YOU. A guy came yesterday and delivered some boxes to your room so you should be all set up."

"My dad owns a trucking business," I blurted. "But he has a small car. And with the burns. It was just cheaper than. Anyway." I don't know why I felt the sudden need to explain why I wasn't lugging my stuff around like everyone else. The idea of having something delivered to me suddenly made me feel like a snob. Or an invalid. An invalid snob.

An invalid snob with a neck full of disgusting scabs. A person worthy of continued, possibly never-ending, mockery and isolation.

You get the idea.

Loading a stack of pamphlets, glossy pieces of photocopied neon paper, and a bright pink Dylan Hall PRIDE shirt onto my one free arm, Joy did her best not to make eye contact with my scabs as she breezed through the rest of her spiel. I did my best to keep my body angled so that she couldn't glance up and stare at my neck.

"OKAY! *SO*, this wristband gets you into all the frosh events, including the concert and the first-year BBQ PIT, so don't take it off. This week is REZSTOCK so there's tons of stuff to do. Tomorrow there's a Dylan Hall Bagel Breakfast and a run up Mount Joseph at seven a.m. sharp. Then there's a Hall Meeting at noon and a campus tour and scavenger hunt at eleven a.m. SHARP. Then there's the campus concert at eight. Are you a big hip-hop fan?"

"Sure."

"Okay great, Allison!" Joy beamed, already grabbing another bracelet for the next victim. "WELCOME TO DYLAN!"

"Right. Bye."

As the line behind me pushed forward, I swivelled and attempted to plunge my way through the crowd, which seemed to have expanded into every available corner of the building like a squealing ocean wave of Dylan Hall residents. After weeks of being bandaged, disinfected on a regular basis, and relatively isolated, I'd completely forgotten how to walk in a crowd and finally resorted to frantically boxing my way forward. By the time I got into the cramped elevator and up to the eleventh floor, I was humming from the overload of physical contact. Racing my way around the U-shaped maze, I found room seven, pushed open the door, and flung myself inside.

Ah the joys of the average dorm room's functional yet in no way comforting decor.

No matter what popular movies about college life
would have you believe, especially movies about
college cheerleaders, the dorm room is basically a
small, cheap-looking hotel room with no bedding
or TV. Smelling faintly of strawberry air freshener.
Space-wise, there's just enough room for the average-
sized student to walk four steps from the door to
the window, turn, and walk back four paces along
the same line. My room contained a small cot with
a canvas-covered mattress, an orange chair, and a
desk-slash-shelving-slash-closet unit. I had one huge,
single-pane window, facing south, and, for some
weird reason, a grand total of four mirrors: one by
the bed, one over the desk, and two on the closet
doors. Funhouses don't have this many mirrors.
Standing alone in my room, I was surrounded by
me. Stacked up on the far wall were several boxes of
my stuff. If I wasn't clear whether I was in the right
place, there was my name written multiple times in
my mother's sharply angled font.

ALLISON LEE—Clothes

ALLISON LEE—Bedding

ALLISON LEE—Books

Wow. Looks like ALLISON LEE IS HERE.

Staring at this tower of mom-handled stuff, I had
a sudden urge to hug my possessions. I was acting

on this urge, my face pressed against a strip of tape, when there was a knock on the door.

"Hello?" I called, not really wanting to do much more than that.

"Uh. Hi!"

There was a long pause. "Um. Okay. Are you going to open the door?"

Outside my room a small tribe of fellow eleventh-floor residents stood behind a tiny doll-like girl with pink and blond hair in what appeared to be a matching pink and yellow athletic top and skirt. Grinning from ear to ear, she stuck out her tiny hand, revealing a foamy pink bangle and pink nails. She looked like someone auditioning for the role of a cheerleader on a family sitcom.

"Hi! I'm Carly."

"Allison." I took her little hand and shook it. Carly's handshake pulsed with the energy level of someone who you would imagine drank a lot of caffeine.

Spreading her other arm out, Carly pointed to the crew behind her. "This is Mary and Karen and … June." Mary, Karen, and June, in jeans and T-shirts, looked like a drab denim backdrop behind Carly. "We're, um, rooms two, three, four, and eight? Everyone's going downstairs for pizza in the common. You want to come get to know your fellow floormates?" Mary, Karen, and June waved.

There is no such noun. Floormates. Fake noun.

"Yah-no," I chuckled, leaning into the door frame and dropping Carly's hand, trying to sound and appear uninterested but not necessarily rude. "Actually. I was just unpacking." Unpacking, feeling weird and out of place, same thing.

"Oh! Um, right," Carly chirped. "You just got here, huh? Okay well, you should come down and join us when you're done!"

I could feel the edge of Karen's gaze scanning, accessing, settling like a mosquito on my neck.

Shifting my left side out of view, I tried not to scowl (while no doubt scowling away). "Sure," I said. Affirmative and yet noncommittal. The best word ever.

Carly did a little jump backward into the hall, like someone preparing to do a cartwheel. "Coolio. We'll see you in a bit!"

I threw out fast handshakes to Mary, Karen, and June and then (quickly) closed the door.

A little over an hour of being a girl with my own place and already I had an assortment of nosy neighbours.

Another hour later, as I was curled up on the bed reading, another knock came.

There was Carly, alone, standing with her hand on her hip.

"So, um. Okay. Not to be rude. But. Is it because of your burns," she asked, "that you're not coming downstairs? Are you, like, nervous or something? About people being uncomfortable. Or something?"

"Oh! No." God, I thought, just go away. "I just, you know, I was just kind of sitting in my room. Just unpacking. Like I said." I could feel my high-school-hostile nerves pricking up and waving in the non-existent breeze.

Carly took a small step into my room and looked around with an air of practical optimism I would eventually come to admire.

"Okay," she said finally, and then, carefully choosing and spacing out her words, "I guess I just figured I'd come up and see if maybe I could hook you into coming down. I mean, you know, it's orientation week." The sparsely decorated surfaces of my room slid past her gaze: my bare-looking bed with its oatmeal-coloured sheets, my computer with its fuzzy-TV screensaver, my stack of black journals piled up on the desk.

Not your typical teen dream mansion.

"Maybe I'm … maybe I'm just not much of an orientation-week person," I shrugged, stating the obvious.

Taking a step backward, Carly tilted her head and looked sad and suddenly still.

"Oh um, right. I guess, you know, I thought maybe I'd just come up and see. I mean, maybe you could just come down for one slice?"

Clearly, this monster called orientation was a stickier beast than the phenoms of high school: physical education class, overnight camp spirit week, Halloween—all things I'd managed to detour in past years through a complex system of avoidance and denial.

I think the problem with orientation week, narrowing it down, is that even if it is a fake holiday, a college creation, people believe it's real. It's like Santa Claus: everyone knows he's not an actual ambassador of Christmas, and yet we all get a thrill out of pretending we don't. The people who make the biggest show of believing are the people with the most spirit. People who refuse to hang stockings by the chimney, on the other hand, are really sad or assholes.

My refusal to take part in frosh was obviously making Carly … sad?

Why it didn't make her think I was just an asshole is anyone's guess. I suppose that after several years of having people read my silence as some sign of asshole-ness, I was kind of touched by that.

"You know what," I said, after what must have been a long silence, "I'm done. Putting things away I mean."

"Seriously? Yay!" Carly chirped. "There's pizza and if you hurry you can get a slice in before we go up to Alpha Delta Phi. There's a concert thing too but a bunch of us are going to skip out and go to Alpha."

I half expected Carly to reach for my hand like some sort of camp counsellor, but instead she did a jump-turn and walked out the door to the elevator.

As we waited for it I casually leaned on the fire extinguisher case, pretending not to be reading the instructions, while Carly whistled the opening lines to what sounded like an old game-show theme song.

"What's Alpha?" I finally asked.

"The fraternity?" Carly hopped through the rickety elevator doors (which had evidently been painted and then scratched up on a yearly basis). "For the party?"

Clearly, I was about to fail my very first college cool test.

"Is it like an all-ages thing? Or. Just. Because I don't have, uh, ID. I mean, I HAVE ID but I don't have …"

"Fake ID."

"Yeah."

"What do you use to go to bars at home?"

FAIL.

"Um, I don't really. I'm."

Well, let's see. You don't need fake ID to go to the movies so … it's never really been a problem.

Finally I stuttered, "I skipped a year in junior high … so. I'm even … younger. Just, uh."

I watched as the gears in Carly's brain clicked forward. "Right. You know what? Don't worry about it. I got this."

On the main floor, the quivering mass of women I'd pushed through earlier had concentrated into a solid block of the newly arrived. As I walked through the corridor lined with framed pictures of Dylan Hall in earlier (black and white) days of tennis and posh picnics (apparently), the hum of their voices was not unlike a hive of angry bees—except there was laughing. So a hive of laughing bees, if that's possible.

In the main common area, outfitted with a fancy flat-screen TV and functional oak and green-upholstered furniture, girls of all shapes and sizes in various positions between standing and sitting chatted and reached across each other for pizza.

Stepping over a pizza box and a cluster of floormates, Carly headed toward the centre of the room, and I followed.

In case you're wondering, a room of giggling freshman-year dorm residents is not unlike any other room of giggling girls. It is not, in and of itself, a scary or intimidating thing, unless, of course, you know a little something about the individual particles of the girls who make up these masses.

My parents sent me to my first all-girls' school in grade six after a boy in grade seven attacked a girl in my class behind the music portable. With a clarinet. She was fine, eventually, but it totally shook up my parents (who spent years checking to see if residual memories of the horrific incident had stuck in my brain). After that, I suppose, it just seemed to be a good idea to continue the trend, and so my parents sent me to an all-girls' overnight camp and, later, a horseback riding camp that allowed boys, although few came. As a result, my young memories of teenage boys are fleeting and grainy, focused on cousins and the tall but sickly boy who lived across the street from me until his parents moved to

Hong Kong. When I think of boys, I think of either birthdays or Halloween; boys were a holiday thing for me, is essentially what I'm saying.

A life spent in this kind of environment is going to be either a surefire path to homosexuality or a surefire deterrent.

I'm into girls, but I have some pretty strong reservations about this decision on my heart's part. For me, "lesbianism," if you want to call it that (I hate that word), is like a kind of physical betrayal, like Tourette syndrome. It's like, why, given my MANY experiences with the claws and fangs of girls, would I decide to put myself on the path of pursuing them for the rest of my life? It's shocking to me that I could fall in love with a girl, let alone more than one girl. Although, you know, let's not exclude the possibility that some boy will come along and sweep me off my feet. Boys, it seems, are just so cool and everyone wants one. Why not me?

By the time I joined the circle of girls from the eleventh floor, talk had moved to the subject of boyfriends and who had them. Most did. Of my floormates, June, Mary, this girl Katy, and Karen all had boyfriends, all attending other schools. Missy, who had roughly the same proportions as a Cabbage Patch doll (was I the tallest on my floor at five-five?), carried a little white old-lady purse, and wore her hair in long black braids, had a boyfriend at the

technical college just on the other side of town. The
boyfriend was living in an apartment downtown
instead of a residence. So, clearly, this would be
the last time any of us saw Missy. Everyone except
this girl Hope, also the only girl in coveralls, was in
the arts program and so, after hometown and more
boyfriend information was exchanged, we settled
into the comfortable topic of potential classes. I was
seriously reconsidering just about every class I'd
signed up for by the time girls started standing up
and moving out.

"Where are we going?"

"Frat party," Hope whispered.

"Right."

Outside, Carly appeared waving a white card in her
hand.

"TA-DA! ID!"

A small group circled to check the match.

"Trick is to find one of the older super geeky students
who stays in residence forever," Hope noted. "They,
like, NEVER go out."

"Allison Lee," Carly pronounced, holding the card
up in the air like a superhero, "I hereby do ... uh ...
name? No. Okay. I do hereby CHRISTEN you, uh,
Jennifer Taylor. Jennifer is the older sister of Grace

Taylor, who's on the sixth floor. Okay? Just put your finger over the picture when you show them the card if they ask."

"Which they probs won't," Mary said. "These guys never check ID. Obviously because they want young and cute chicks like us to party with."

"Wow. That's so awesome," Missy breathed, leaning in to check out my score. "It's so much better than mine. Look. Mine looks like I got it at the 7-Eleven or something."

"Dude, I bought mine on the internet," Hope added. "Whatever. As long as the hair colour matches. That's all that matters."

"What did I tell you, right?" Carly smiled. "No problem. Let's GO!"

Jennifer Taylor's eyes were wider apart than mine. And she had nicer eyebrows. Our hair was pretty similar, though. I gripped the ID just so, covering her face enough that her bangs framed the crescent of my thumbnail.

"I am Jennifer Taylor."

Trudging up the hill to Alpha Delta Phi under a Pixar-starry sky, Carly, Missy, and I linked arms and leaned into the incline. I don't think I'd ever linked arms with more than one person and walked any distance before. It was less cumbersome than I'd imagined. As Carly's body jostled close to mine, I was suddenly hit with the knowledge of the most obvious element of freshman year, which is that in freshman year, you can be anything you want to be.

That's not exactly true; obviously, there are SOME THINGS you cannot be. Like, no, you can't pretend to be a movie star because people will more than likely know you're NOT a movie star. And no, obviously, you can't pretend to be tall, or beautiful, if you're not.

That's not what I'm saying.

I'm saying that I realized, with Jennifer Taylor's ID tucked in my back pocket, that the people I was walking with knew almost nothing about me: we knew each other's names, and by the time we left Dylan Hall I had most of my floormates' cell numbers in my phone and they had mine (for emergencies). On top of that, my floormates knew:

» that I was seventeen years old

» that I had graduated from a private girls' school

» that I didn't have a boyfriend

» and that I was an arts major.

Beyond that, Hope knew I was a fan of both techno music and old-school rock and roll (and I knew Hope liked metal, in part because she had a "METAL" tattoo in big gooey letters on her bicep). Everyone knew I'd burned myself at one point in the summer, although no one knew how or why. I just said I'd been in an accident.

But that's it.

So for a brief moment in time I was in the freshman threshold of opportunity: the people around me knew only what I'd told them about myself. Nothing more. They'd had almost no time to formulate an opinion for themselves and no one was around to inform them of anything different from what I said or what I did. If I smiled and giggled at their jokes, I could be a happy-go-lucky person. If I slept with the first boy I laid eyes on, I could be a slut. I could even get in a fight and be a loose cannon or a bully.

The world was my oyster.

THREE

The tower of power

College, and especially the freshman-year portion of
the undergrad college career, is kind of like Europe:
on the one hand it has all these associations with
tradition and old buildings, culture and stuff. La la
la. On the other hand there's places like, what's it
called, Amsterdam, you know, parts of Europe where
if you go people know you're only going there to
party.

Not that there's anything wrong with that.

The TOWER OF POWER, held by the Alpha Delta
fraternity, was not an official St. Joseph's freshman
event, but it was definitely the most popular amongst
the ready-to-party freshman students.

Legend has it the TOWER OF POWER was dreamed
up by the Alpha Delta brothers after they moved
into a new building with five floors of frat goodness.

The goal of the TOWER was to make sure girls visited all five floors, giving more dudes on more floors more opportunities to score. The rules were simple. Visitors got a set of plastic shot glasses at the door and were supposed to visit each floor for a "specialty" shot (each floor was responsible for organizing a bartender and supplies). Brothers who wanted to keep party-goers happy decorated their floor to go with the theme of their shot.

That night the menu was:

First floor: CEMENT MIXER SPECIAL
Second Floor: ATOMIC FIREBALL
Third Floor: ACID DROP
Fourth Floor: PINK PANTHER
Fifth Floor: FRESHMAN BRAIN ERASER
+ beer*
(*that's a pretty key element to this story actually)

Back in the day, all the shots were called, like, Blow Job and Panty Waster, with a handful of ethnic shots that had racist names no one I talked to that night could remember. I guess the fraternity council, fearing a lawsuit, said the night would be scrapped if they didn't come up with some way to keep it sounding less XXX. So now the shots were really fruity and slightly more poetic. To avoid "excessive drunkenness," fraternity seniors were supposed to keep an eye on younger students to make sure things didn't get out of hand. Plus, the idea was, with a max of one shot per floor, students could avoid excessive drinking.

Right.

Of course, these kinds of parties are hardly ever orderly events that follow any kind of rule. By the time we lined up at the double doors of the house, word had spread that the way to avoid the one-shot rule was to grab as many shot glasses as possible while drunken frat boys made a show of (seemingly randomly) checking IDs. One guy wearing plastic goggles (like the kind they handed out in chemistry labs) even had the foresight to bring his own bag of shot glasses, which seemed a little insane and kind of nerdy to me at the time, but I guess that guy got super laid that night so there it is: foresight is sexy.

The place was a zoo. I'm not saying that to be stereotypical and I recognize that it's kind of a worn-out metaphor for describing large crowds, but at the same time, if the shoe fits ... By ten-thirty the air was thick with bodies and music as people packed around the first makeshift bar to get their little cups filled with what looked like stale latte mix poured by two super tall boy bartenders in construction hats.

A herd of guys in navy blue ALPHA, BABY! T-shirts crushed their shot glasses against their foreheads and pounded each other on the chest.

Crick, crack. Thump thump thump thump!

"TO-WER of POW-ER!"

After swallowing the first shot, everyone headed for the stairs and started scrambling up to the next floor. Girls screamed and boys hollered like unrehearsed warriors charging onto the field.

Surprisingly, everything was going pretty smoothly for the first hour or so. Moving from floor to floor, I tried to absorb, but not get crushed by, the raging mass of students. As increasingly puffy and increasingly drunk faces zoomed into my space, I tried to make comments that were not anti-social sounding. Mostly I said stuff like, "What's the shot here?" and "This shot is not bad actually." I think I even had a handful of fairly lucid conversations until my impromptu crew of alcohol-swilling new friends hit the third floor, which residents had covered in neon yellow construction paper. On my fourth contraband shot of Acid Drop, my sixth shot of the night (plus beer), I felt a sudden internal loss of gravity. Lurching into the nearest room, I did a massive, somewhat projectile, lemony upchuck into someone's Bugs Bunny garbage pail.

Mostly into someone's Bugs Bunny garbage pail.

Anyway.

By the time I found Carly and Missy and June again, I was woozy and they were on their fourth Pink Panthers. Popping her shot glass out of her mouth like it was a ping-pong ball, Carly threw her hands up in the air, sending dribbles of the leftovers from her glass flying.

"TOWER OF POWER!" she cheered.

"TO THE TOWER!" someone else shouted.

"THIS LOOKS LIKE PEPTO-BISMOL!" I yelled. Pretending it was, I imagined the cool liquid coating my stomach and made a silent promise not to throw up in anyone else's garbage can. I felt pretty guilty about the whole thing. "THIS IS NOT BAD ACTUALLY!"

Until about ten minutes later.

As we moved toward the stairs and the music changed from techno to rock, I caught sight of Missy out of the corner of my eye ... covering her mouth.

I'm sure you can guess what happened next.

So, as it turns out, the other name for the TOWER OF POWER is the TOWER OF PUKE. This is what happens to the Tower of Power when people do the Tower of Power more than once, do more than one shot at each level of the tower, or drink too much beer (and do the Tower of Power).

I think the name pretty much speaks for itself.

The real disaster zone was the stairs.

Missy's Pink Panther had lasted all of five minutes before she rocket-vomited on the landing between four and five (and it wasn't pink, surprisingly, but orange). Carly upchucked a rainbow of alcoholic delights between three and four, where we met up with several other boys and girls puking their way up and down the stairs. The movie reference, if you're looking for one, is Steven Spielberg's *Stand By Me* (a film that would be assigned in my Cultural Studies class). Fortunately for me, I'm mostly a one-time puker. Unfortunately for me, it hardly mattered, since by the time we made it outside, Carly had thrown up on me.

"Fuuuuck," she slurred, "iz it in yer burns?"

"Nope," I slurred back, "but I'm gonna go home anyway."

"You mean to rez."

"Yeah."

"WAIT!" Regaining her balance by leaning forward like an Olympic swimmer about to leap into a first lap, Carly huffed for a moment before righting herself and pointing down the hill. "We're coming with you."

By "we," of course, she meant her and Missy, although Missy was already sitting on the steps outside and curled forward like a little kid contemplating a somersault.

"I think I need to call my boyfriend," she whimpered and then fell forward onto her face and threw up again.

"Fuck!" Dropping down to her knees, Carly grabbed Missy's cell phone, carefully wiping the vomit-splashed case with her sleeve. "Just go, Allison. You should, uh, clean off your neck. We'll see you later, okay?"

"Okay."

As I slumped away from what was sounding and, I'm sure, looking like a gut-soaked version of Wild Water Kingdom, the mayhem continued. I passed herds of girls in various throwing-up poses. Dodging around a puddle of puke, I nearly fell over a blond girl kneeling on the road.

"WATCH IT," she snapped.

"Sorry."

"Fuck. Do you see a lighter anywhere? It's blue."

"Oh." Looking down, it was pretty easy to spot. "It's in this pile of puke," I said, pointing.

"Of course." Bumping through her pockets for a spare, the girl seemed to get a good look at me. "Leave your friends at the party?" she asked.

"I don't have any friends," I slurred.

Which at the time was, technically, true. Or a leftover sentiment from high school stuck to my brain like so much old gum.

I turned to leave and she stood up. "What's your name?"

"Allison."

Discovering another lighter in her back pocket, the girl grinned. "Goodnight, Allison."

She didn't say her name. She just looked at me and walked away.

I wobbled back to residence with this thought in my head: that the girl I'd just met was beautiful.

I didn't know that this person whose lighter I'd spotted in a pile of puke was Shar. Shar Sinclair. Future best friend and soon to be brand-new biggest mistake.

How would I possibly know that?

I was drunk and covered in puke.

FOUR

And you are

It took a while to get used to sleeping in a new bed, in part because the beds at Dylan were two feet wide and soft like a bird's nest made of barbed wire, and in part because sleeping at Dylan Hall on the eleventh floor meant waking up to Metallica. At full blast. Every morning.

The source of Metallica was Hope, who at seven a.m. liked to start her day with an explosion of music by angry men. Sometimes she'd even prop her door open with a garbage can so she could hear the music while she showered in the bathroom across the hall. My first three mornings at Dylan Hall went something like this:

7:00 a.m.—ENTER METALLICA.

5 seconds later—Slam knee on concrete wall waking up to blast of Metallica.

5 seconds later—Have delirious moment of wondering where the fuck I am and why Metallica is also there and why they are so fucking loud.

20 seconds later—Lie in bed surrounded by the screams and groans of eleventh-floor residents and think about Anne.

My first "girlfriend."

I'm actually still not sure whether or not to call her that.

That's stupid but that's reality. Every time—even every, like, "mental" in-my-head time—I call her my "girlfriend," I still feel a little pinch.

The first few seconds after waking up was a pretty potent time for thinking about Anne because of this memory I have from the morning after the first and only time she ever slept over, also the morning after the first and only time I ever slept with a girl, when she rolled over and looked at me and said, "It's you."

That's what I used to see over and over again whenever I daydreamed or closed my eyes or sat down or heard any song by a woman sung in a breathy voice: Anne's face pressed against my pillow, her sleepy eyes opening, eyelashes fluttering back to reveal cool blue eyes, irises focusing on me.

Anne's little pink lips folding over her words,
"It's you."

What's that saying? About how you don't know
you want something until you have it and it's taken
away? Is it the one about the eggs?

I don't know.

I also didn't know at the time that Anne woke
up every morning not knowing where she was or
thinking she was somewhere she wasn't. Apparently,
the morning she woke up in my room, she thought
she was at her grandma's house—partly because of
my flowery sheets.

When she said "It's you," I thought she meant, like,
"You're the one. It's you." "It's you" was the most
amazing thing I'd ever heard anyone say when it
came from Anne's mouth. The words felt like a breath
of perfect cold winter air. It wasn't until a week later,
between first and second period, that I heard about
the grandma thing and the waking up stuff.

"So what did you mean when you said 'It's you'?" I
asked.

"Duh! I meant, like, not my grandma!" Anne scoffed,
I would say overly defensively. "What did you think
I meant?"

What did she think I thought it meant?

I wanted to say that the grandma thing was messed up considering what we'd done to each other the night before, but I didn't.

I can't imagine what thoughts Metallica inspired in the other people on the eleventh floor. I'm pretty sure they weren't very, uh, positive thoughts.

Mostly people screamed at Hope to "SHUT THE FUCKING MUSIC OFF." Or just to "FUCK OFF."

A more delicate approach was taken by Katy, my next-door neighbour, a social work student with a frizzy perm and plans to get her degree, return home, and marry her boyfriend of eight years (which meant they'd gotten together when they were in grade school). Katy had a pad of sticky notes on which she would write long and involved messages to Hope about the "best interests of the floor."

I don't think Hope read Katy's notes. She didn't even bother to peel them off her door. As an engineering student, for the first week of school she had a million frosh activities to go to, some of which involved painting herself red, many of which involved running around with the rest of the engineering students from sun-up to sundown. So I almost never saw her. I probably couldn't even tell you Hope's eye colour, but if you gave me a keyboard I could recreate the opening of "Enter Sandman" for you. Now and possibly for the rest of my life.

You'd think there'd be some sort of administrative solution to something like a morning heavy-metal wake-up call. I mean, you know, there were all these brochures on college life and LIVING IT UP IN RESIDENCE, plus we sat through this three-hour snooze-fest "Welcome to Dylan Hall" orientation meeting the second day, where all the floorfellows got up and talked to us about how following the rules would make everyone's life better.

That meeting was one of many events I ended up going to with Carly. After barfing on me, she seemed to think it was her responsibility to make sure I had someone to go to things with. Before heading out just about anywhere, most especially to a meal, she'd knock on my door.

"Hey you! You wanna go get some grub?"

Carly wasn't like anyone I'd hung out with for a very long time, partly because I didn't hang out with a very wide selection of people. For one thing, she was always really fucking happy. Happy in the way a child who knows nothing of sorrow is happy. Happy in a way that radiated out of her face and clothes and hair. The first day I met her I guessed she'd never broken a bone and I was right. The girl was, like, born in sunshine or something. Sometimes, instead of walking, she would bounce down the stairs and then land at the bottom with a swivel turn.

The other amazing thing about Carly was that, despite her intensive happiness, she did not appear to be stupid. I used to have this theory that happiness was oblivion, you know? So in order to be happy you had to be able to block out reality. Carly, on the other hand, seemed to have a pretty firm grip on the world around her. Like she had this insane ability to remember everything anyone ever told her. By the end of the first week she knew everyone's name, floor, and what classes they were in, even if they had no connection to what Carly was taking. It was like walking around with a human Google search page, or a mom. Every five minutes it was like, "Oh look, there's _____."

Sample:

Carly: Oh look, there's Sandy.

Me: Sandy. Sandy? The girl with the slightly infected nose pierce?

Carly: Uh. Ew! No! Sandy. She's on the ninth floor. From Indiana?

Me: Yeah. I think. Yeah. With the nose pierce and the slight BO? Who's in East Asian History?

Carly: Oh my gosh, you're SO FUNNY.

I am not a human memory stick so I typically didn't know who Carly was talking about. In fact, I think

the only time we ever did zero in on the same girl
was in Cultural Studies, which just about every first-
year student was enrolled in, when Carly leaned over
and said, "There's Sharon."

She was pointing at the girl I vaguely recognized
from our hazy, barfy, lighter-searching encounter
after the Tower of Power.

"Sharon?"

"Sharon. Or, wait, Shar? No, it's Shar. She's on the
sixth floor. I think she's friends with that Asian girl
in the stretch pants."

"Who? Where?"

Carly pointed with her pinky.

Shar.

As the majority of the class leaned forward in
the McDonald's-like bucket seats of the Leacock
auditorium, conceivably to hear the thin strains
of the prof's instructions coming through the
classroom's ancient speakers, Shar, sitting several
rows over and dressed entirely in black, skin-tight
clothing, leaned back, flicked her hair over her
shoulder, and yawned. Like a fat cat on a windowsill.

I'm trying to think of the best way to describe Shar
to you without using words like "beautiful" and
"model," which are accurate but not helpful. She

had a tiny body and a large round head framed by blond hair. Her skin was ivory white, glowing at the edges of her black collar. From a distance she looked like an ad, like someone who existed only as a visual representation of something expensive. I briefly considered the possibility that she was a movie star or something. Movie stars go to college too, right?

Suggesting that Shar might be a movie star was one of the first embarrassing moments of my college career, which is sad considering I'd managed to get through the Tower of Power (almost) incident-free.

"A MOVIE STAR?" Carly cackled, in a rare moment of disbelief, biting into the soft jelly-like middle of her Dylan Hall cafeteria mystery dessert. "Okay. You are SOOO FUNNY!"

"Forget it. What time is it anyway? I think I have class."

"One oh four."

Social Problems. One-thirty p.m. Main hall.

Of all the courses I was forced and happy to take my freshman year, probably the one cool one was Social Problems. Social Problems had me at "hello." I mean, first of all, it was a class that's about current events and fricking craziness, wars and riots and all that. It was a class all about fucking up, like, on a large scale. Had to connect to me somehow, right? Second of all, the professor was hilarious.

Professor Jawari moved with what you might describe as a vampire-like, uncanny lightning speed. She streaked from the auditorium door to the lecture podium in a blink. It was incredibly difficult to track her movements. She just appeared.

"Okay, miscreants," she barked our first day, towering over the lectern like a wizard or maybe a mythical beast that's really tall. "This is Social Problems, this is not a cheese course, I have no patience for kids surfing the net in my class, so shut your laptops NOW. Like right NOW. HEY! I'm teaching. If you're here I want you HERE. Okay? I'm not your mom so don't make me sound like your mom by making me repeat myself a MILLION TIMES. NOW!"

A series of laptop clicks echoed across the crowd of hundreds of seated course-shoppers. Many students mouthed, in mock horror, "MOM?"

Professor Jawari squinted. "My name is Professor Jawari. You can call me Professor J, although, technically, this is a first-year class and none of you should have any reason to call me. This is not a class for lecturing, this is a class with questions, because the social sciences, of which this is one, involve QUESTIONING and so I will ask questions. A lot of questions. If any of this scares you I would suggest you get the heck out of here now, before I waste a dead tree on you with one of these here OUTlines."

The woman was crazy like a talk show host. Like one of those judges on one of those TV court shows.

It was amazing.

More people should talk like this, I thought. It would make life way more interesting.

About forty kids got up and left before she was even finished speaking. She waved them off then chugged a bottle of what looked like energy drink.

With a mass of sweatshirts and bodies removed, I noticed Shar sitting in the front row, her stiletto boot dangling out into the aisle.

Thirty minutes into the class, everyone noticed Shar.

"Okay. So, for example, name one social problem you would obliterate if you could," Professor J had challenged.

"War!" someone called out.

"Violence," someone else added.

"Poverty."

"Racism."

"Violence against women."

"Television," someone else offered.

"Capitalism," the massive hippie with the beard next to me called out.

"Obesity," someone behind me interrupted, ignoring the hands-up rule.

Shar must have yawned. Professor J bent over her lectern and looked at her, zeroed in on her.

"And you?" she asked. "What's your big contribution?"

Shar's voice was sharp and clear, a clean note amongst the fuzz of that much space. "Nothing," she said.

"Not going to stand in the way of any world-altering problems?" Professor J persisted.

"No."

"Just going to relax and watch the carnage unfold?"

"Of course."

At the back of the room, a boy dressed in a top hat and a trench coat laughed loudly and clapped.

Professor J also chuckled, slamming her lecture book closed. "Okay, on that note, that's it for today. Don't be morons. Do the reading and I'll see you next week."

Carly was waiting in the hall under a WELCOME banner with a handful of free-for-student snacks. Apparently a bunch of people were outside dressed as chip bags, juggling snacks and throwing them at passing students.

"This is why we're all going to get huge," I observed, slamming a handful of chicken-flavoured bagel bits in my mouth. "Freshman fatteners."

"Not if we join that morning jog group," Carly noted.

As we munched, I noticed that the top hat guy had grabbed a seat on the floor in the centre of the hallway and become a human road bump as the crowd swirled around him. Under his top hat he had huge eyebrows and, from what I could see, some skin problems that rivalled what was happening on my neck.

"That guy's in my class." I nodded in his direction.

"Hey! I like his hat. What's his name?"

"Dunno."

By the time we got to our ravioli dinner that night in the Dylan Hall cafeteria, the big story was that, shortly after we left, some guy had broken his arm tripping over top hat guy. This was pretty bad news because the guy who tripped was a basketball player. I guess a lot of people were pretty pissed. This girl from my floor, Mary, said that the top hat guy ran off before the paramedics got there and some other students dragged him back to apologize.

"Dragged?"

"Totally DRAGGED. Like, apparently, he ran really far, too."

"What's his NAME?" Carly asked.

No one knew.

"He's in Allison's class," Carly added.

"Really?" Mary asked.

"Yeah. Social Problems."

"I heard that class is all crazy hard and the teacher is a psycho."

I shrugged.

"I also heard that this girl was in there saying she approved of genocide."

"That's not what she said," I mumbled, stabbing my stale ravioli and trailing it through the ketchup-tomato sauce coating my plate. "She just didn't have anything she'd like to eradicate."

"A pacifist," someone else I didn't recognize observed.

"No."

Funny the things we know before we actually know them.

Months later, when our friendship became a topic of conversation, Shar would say that we were sitting together in that first Social Problems class.

"No, I was sitting next to a hippie in a beard who was against money," I corrected. "We met at film club."

Of course, it's not really important that the first time I actually spoke more than a handful of words to Shar was several days after that first class, at the first meeting of the Film Appreciation Society (which later wouldn't be called that). But it was, for a long time, what I considered to be our first meeting.

It was Carly's idea to go. I guess she heard some other girls talking about it at lunch and totally fell in love with the idea. At the time we were doing pretty much everything together, so I decided to go too. I'm not huge into film but, you know, why not? I thought maybe we could watch a bunch of free movies.

The film group itself was dreamed up by this guy named Boris Borlau, if you can believe it, a hand talker who wore, among other things, a charcoal turtleneck and a pair of Ray-Ban shades perched in his crown of thick, curly black hair. Guy looked like Bob Dylan. Carly and I sat next to the clearly gay guys in the clearly gay fuzzy sweaters and hair full of product. The gay guys were all talking about Stanley Kubrick and Wes Anderson, although I couldn't tell exactly what they were saying. The rest of the people in the group, all blondes, were talking about some band when Shar slipped in the room and grabbed a chair. As she calmly untangled herself from her scarf, Boris clapped his hands.

"Okay, so, hey guys. Welcome to the Film Appreciation Society. Right. I'm really glad you're all here and it's, uh, great to see so many people with an interest in film. I guess we should start by going around and introducing ourselves. Maybe say what your favourite film genre is and who you are? I'll start: I'm Boris and my favourite film genre would have to be film noir."

"I'm Judy, I'm also really into film noir."

"I'm Tanya. Hello. And I would also have to say film noir actually. Guess we're just a bunch of darkies."

Ha ha, whoops.

"Oh. Okay. Hello, dolls. I'm Danny. I generally adhere to the auteur system so my genre would be better described as Kubrickian. But let's not make a big deal about it."

"I'm Carly, I'm into musicals." Carly twirled her finger in the air when she said "musicals."

Eyes pivoted to focus on me. I was still trying to figure out what "genre" my favourite films were. Which meant trying to figure out exactly what was meant by "genre."

"Um. I'm Allison. And. Um."

Across the room, Shar shifted in her seat, recrossed her legs, and smiled at me. "Horror?" she asked, tapping at her neck in the same place where my scar was.

Next to me I could hear the sound of Carly's mouth popping open.

There was an instant stillness in the room, broken only by the mouselike coffee-slurping of a guy in an orange sweater. Shar tilted her head, widened her eyes at me. Smiled.

I froze, could feel my body seizing up, a sensation similar to what any kind of prey feels when encountered by a predator. A familiar sensation, not unlike what I felt stepping into every gym class I attended from grades nine to twelve.

I remember looking at Shar, her face a mask of amusement. She was looking directly back at me, like someone getting ready to pass a note, or a secret.

As someone who was distinctly unpopular and picked on in high school, I've often felt it should be

easier to interpret the things other people do and
say more accurately, more often. There should be a
system of language that lets us know not only what
people mean but also the level of hostility implied.
Imagine how lovely all our childhoods would be if
we knew that sort of thing, if we knew the difference
between a person being vicious and a person
attempting to be friendly. Like the time Rahnuma
Tang, from across the street, invited me to a birthday
party that didn't exist, luring me into her backyard
so that I could get jumped by a bunch of her crappy
friends who beat me with their skipping ropes,
almost blinding me in the process. I know there
are some people who see sound as colour, and I've
always wondered if mean looks different than not
mean. I bet it's purple.

"Um. Right," I said, slowly crawling into my
sentence the way you step into a shoe after you've
just seen a cockroach on the floor, "totally horror."

Slurp. Sip.

Shar's smile spread across her face. She reached
a finger into her blond hair and twisted herself a
temporary band around her index finger. As she
grinned, a warm glow of relief spread across my
limbs.

"And you?" Boris asked, leaning forward and
pointing at Shar.

"Oh," she said, in a somewhat mocking singsong voice, not looking at him, "I'm Shar and I'll watch anything as long as Julia Roberts isn't in it."

After the meeting, as the group exchanged numbers and emails, I was sitting alone in my folding chair when Shar slipped over beside me. Up close, her black outfit revealed several shades of black: jet, ink, and coal and steel, fuzzy, and velvet all wrapped together. Her perfume curled through the air, snaking a faint trail of what smelled like hot pink orchids around my head.

"Shar Sinclair," she said.

"Allison Lee," I replied.

"Sooooo, Allison," she said, "you here to make a movie?"

"Uh, no. You?"

"Fuck no," Shar hissed, turning to re-survey the crowd, which appeared to be engaged in a series of intense conversations (about film). "I just dropped in to check out a bunch of losers with delusions of fame."

"Oh. I guess, uh, fun. Sounds fun."

"Do you want to be famous, Allison?" Shar tipped her head forward as though to pour the contents of her eyes into my soul.

"What?"

"Famous, Allison. FAMOUS. Big time. I'm asking if you want to be a STAR."

"No. I mean, no, I don't think so."

"You should know." She raised an eyebrow. It was strange to be the sudden focus of someone like Shar's full attention. It was like being locked into something. Like, a laser beam. A big starship laser beam. "Most people know if they want to be famous. It's a pretty basic thing to know."

"Well I'm not really all that basic, I mean ... right now."

"You don't say."

"I do say."

"Good answer, Allison. Very good answer. You heading back to dorm?"

"Yeah, I just have to wait for Carly."

"Oh, right. CARLY."

On the walk back, wedged between me and Carly, Shar turned and asked her the fame question.

"Doesn't everyone want to be famous? I guess I want to be good famous. Maybe a little famous anyway,"

Carly reflected. "But, like, um, productive famous. Like Meryl Streep or Janeane Garofalo."

Bad answer, apparently.

"Rrreally." Turning her head toward me and away from Carly, Shar rolled her eyes.

"Yeah well. Anyway," Carly said, speeding up a bit, "I thought tonight was pretty interesting. I hope we get to make a movie."

"Oh yeah I'm so glad you invited me tonight, Carly," Shar trilled. "So lucky that I ran into you in the hall. Really great time."

At the lights, Carly paused and turned, her lips neatly pressed together. Like she wanted to say something. To me.

"Really," Shar cooed, "great group."

"Well. Okay. I'm glad you had a good time, Shar. I hope you did too, Allison."

"Sure."

In the elevator, Shar said I should come back to her room to study for Social Problems.

What she actually said, to Carly, as she pulled me out at the sixth floor, was, "I'm taking Allison to my room to force her to teach me about Social Problems. Bye, Superstar!"

As the elevator doors closed, pinching off the image of Carly, she turned to me and said, "For the record, I've just saved you from a year of stupid."

On the sixth floor, Shar's floor, the long hallways were littered with girls sprawled out in coloured pyjamas in various patterns from Disney to camouflage; textbooks open, cradling big bowls of popcorn, they lolled around, giggling and reading. The whole floor smelled like a movie theatre. Shar stepped over the rows of legs like they were driftwood, barely paying attention to the voices around us as she slipped into her room and shut the door.

Inside, music was already playing, something low with lots of bass. Throwing the window open, Shar flopped down on the bed and lit a cigarette. The combination of cold air and smoke made the skin on my neck prickle. Not knowing where to sit, I leaned against the closet and tried to seem cool.

"It's so weird that all our rooms are the same," I said finally, when it appeared that Shar was lost in a haze of nicotine and not planning on speaking. "It's like looking at my room, only …"

"Messy" was what I wanted to say.

"… with more red," I came out with instead, because it seemed like a better thing to say to someone I didn't know.

The word "red" seemed to trigger Shar, who suddenly sat up and craned to look at my burns. "Right," she exhaled. Then, "That thing on your neck is fucking crazy. Were you the survivor of a house fire or something, Allison? Were thousands lost and you walked away?"

"No. I mean. It was a small fire. None were lost. Not even me."

"Right. So ... So, what? So you burned yourself?"

"I had an accident with a bonfire-type thing. That I was making. I had a c— Uh. It was an accident."

Stabbing her cigarette out on the edge of the window with one hand, Shar extended her other hand, the inside of her wrist flexed toward me. "Burned myself once as a kid. Put my hand on a stove element. People thought my parents were abusing me. You can still sort of see the scar."

"Scars are cool."

Amazing how a word like "cool" can land like a lame penny falling from your pocket onto a city sidewalk.

"I mean. I think they tell a really interesting story. Which is ... interesting. They're like skin punctuation ..."

Stop talking, Allison.

Shar raised an eyebrow. "I guess you would know, huh, Allison?"

"Yeah."

Shar smiled. "I always think people with scars are the kind of people you want to hang out with, you know? Not so fucking perky all the time."

Flopping back down on the bed, she stretched out and yawned. "I'm so fucking lazy. I don't even feel like reading. You should just read me a chapter or something."

Chapter one, "Defining Social Problems," was about the different approaches people take to studying social problems. There was a bit in there about the cycles of history, which is really about repeating mistakes. Shar fell asleep after the second page.

FIVE

Fast friends

Sitting lazily in the park, cross-legged, perched on a sweater serving as picnic blanket, Shar ran her fingers through the grass as the smoke from her cigarette smouldered in a patch of dirt not far away. All around us were the plastic skins of pilfered snacks. A troop of tai chi seniors made slow movements just north of us. The leaves of the tall trees that lined the park were slowly breaking from their branches and falling, orange, red, and yellow, to the ground.

The perfect day. Autumn chill but not too fall cold. Shar had crawled into my lecture hall to rescue me from East Asian History and now we were well on our way into our third hour of just sitting and talking, which felt infinitely more important than knowing whatever China was before it was China.

A sour cherry candy melted onto my tongue as I tilted my head up to feel the sun on my face and the slight pull of my burn, which was starting to feel less like a burn and more like leather.

"Truth or dare, Allison."

"What?"

"Truth or dare?" Shar raised an eyebrow, a dapple of sun sliding across her face through the tree above.

"Uh, truth?"

"Have you ever given a guy a blow job?"

Stalling, I attempted to appear momentarily distracted by the art of tai chi. Swinging back to the conversation, I stuttered, "Wait. It's a truth about ME?"

"Have you never played this game, Allison, or are you just avoiding the question?"

Yes to both.

A better question might have been whether I'd ever had a BFF to PLAY Truth or Dare with.

Answer: no.

Making and or getting friends has always been kind of a ... struggle for me.

When I was in grade school, all the girls had first, second, and third best friends, positions you might equate to something like president, vice president, and defence secretary of friendship. These positions were always shifting and depended on what seemed to me to be ridiculous and incalculable factors, qualities that could only be assessed by really popular people like Carolyn Tyler. At our school, Carolyn and her best friends were the grade five mafia; you had to check in with them before you bought hair clips or they'd give you endless amount of shit for buying the wrong ones. Carolyn Tyler was beautiful and had a pool and everyone wanted to be her friend.

I did not have a pool.

Before college I managed to have a sum total of two "friends," whose acquisition and (temporary) loyalty both required some form of bribery/sacrifice. In grade six I traded my bike for a third-best friendship with Dawn Martin, but then I accidentally laughed when she fell off the swing and broke her leg. And then I was pretty much first NOT best friend. First UN best friend.

Senior year I used prescription medication to purchase the affections of Anne Craig.

Yes, THAT Anne.

Anne was one of those girls who was super popular almost by default (both her parents had pools). She had these bouncy curls and these big blue eyes. From grades nine to eleven I think we spoke all of two sentences to each other. Then in senior year, in the fall, we both got put on set-painting duty, assigned to Hamlet's castle. Anne was really messed up because this boy she'd given a blow job to had stopped answering her texts (apparently because he was getting "better" blow jobs from the girl who was playing Hamlet's mother). Anne would hyperventilate and burst into hot spells while we were painting. She wanted to take this drug she'd seen on TV to help her feel better but her doctor didn't believe in medicating moods.

"He's such a power freak," Anne moaned.

"My doctor is really chill," I said, dabbing paint on the fireplace we were both supposed to be painting. "He pretty much does whatever I tell him."

Dr. Zygiel, a pushover who'd been writing me notes to get out of gym, for "cramping" reasons, since I was fourteen.

It took me two doctor's visits to get a prescription. I'd heard enough from Anne to know quite a bit about the symptoms of anxiety, and so it was easy to describe them as my own. For good measure I faked an anxiety attack in his office.

I handed the bottle of pills over to Anne the next day.

"Take them. Feel better."

Anne cried and threw her arms around me. That night she invited me over to her dad's condo and we ate spaghetti and took one and a half pills each. I think by then I was kind of in love with her. We were friends for the rest of first term. And it was kind of amazing. Then we were more than friends. Then it was OVER.

Anyway.

Those were pretty much my only two experiences of friendship going into college.

Fortunately, probably the easiest place and time in the world to make friends is a college campus freshman year. The first month at St. Joseph's was a BFF BONANZA. Everyone was going out of their way to make friends and be friends with people. Girls especially. Boys, I don't know, boys always seem to be making friends. But girls, you know, they need an occasion and this was an occasion. It was like a friend sale, with everyone starting from scratch, NEEDING friends, and OH LOOK here's a bunch of kids your own age. People BECAME friends really fast. Like these two girls from Shar's floor: Sarah and Tori. Sarah was this tall Chinese chick with a big long ponytail of jet-black hair and a lot of cartoon character T-shirts and Tori was this little curly haired

redhead with a lot of track pants. By the end of
the first week they'd become this sweatpants-and-
cartoon-T-shirt-wearing posse.

Shar hated Sarah and Tori. Shar said something
about going to the Tower of Power with Sarah, but
I guess she rubbed Shar the wrong way. Whatever
happened, it left a mark. Shar narrowed her eyes
whenever Sarah and Tori walked past us in rez. She
called them "the Patties" because they'd quickly
developed the habit of eating these veggie patty
things they bought at the convenience store around
the corner and then toasted in the communal
kitchen.

"Look, it's *the Patties*."

"Yeah. Their colons must be totally twisted from
eating all that soy."

"That's Asian Patty," Shar said, pointing.

"What's the little one?"

"Mini Patty."

Shar detested the food at the cafeteria too, but her
solution was a little less healthy than the Patties'.
Basically, whenever possible, we ate in one of
the many crappy diner-type places in and around
campus. Eating was probably the only really non-
glamorous thing Shar did. She walked cool and slow

and looked sly and serious. But she ate like someone who was about to have her plate yanked away. Plus she covered just about everything she consumed in a mess of ketchup so that it looked like roadkill. It was kind of gross.

"The Patties are TOTALLY anorexic," Shar said one day while devouring a hamburger special with fries. "Anyone who insists on going to the bathroom WITH someone, that's anorexia."

"Weird. How do you know they weren't just going to the bathroom together like girls do all the time?"

"There's a difference. You can just tell with girls that are precious like that."

Shar said the Patties reminded her of her sister.

"My sister Madison is anorexic."

Madison, I wanted to say, sounds like a hotel.

"Allison, you don't know what it's like living with that kind of reality-TV fucked-up-ness. It's all well and good to feel sorry for people like that until you have to eat with them."

Shar sucked up a french fry and swiped her ketchup lip gloss off with her napkin. In the booth behind her, boys were rapping along with the restaurant radio. Shar paused to roll her eyes. "My parents had to install a widescreen in the kitchen so we wouldn't have to watch Madison lick her hundred calories out of her special teacup every night. That's the fucked-up thing about anorexia, right? It's cute until someone's skin starts losing its elasticity and their gums bleed. Wait. You're not 'rexian are you?"

"No. I mean. Obviously." Actually I was probably exactly the opposite. My whole life my body had had the exact same shape, like a tube of toothpaste. It was hard to get all worked up about a consistency.

"Never, when you're around me, bitch about feeling fat."

Shar's eyes pinched and focused in on me as though to detect any future body image issues I might whine about.

"You really think the Patties are anorexic? They don't look very thin."

"That's how it STARTS, doesn't it?" Shar scoffed. "You have to BE FAT to want to BE THIN, Allison. Now THERE'S a social problem for you."

Ever since the first Social Problems lecture Shar had gotten into the habit of pointing out social problems whenever they appeared in her view. Crowding, littering, mass stupidity, sameness. College was rife with them.

"Is this a social problem you plan to do something about?" I asked.

"If I wanted to," Shar noted.

After lunch, I went to my Introduction to Linguistics class and Shar went to Environmental Geology, a science class designed for arts students. Environmental Geology was composed almost entirely of slackers in sweatshirts who would text on their cell phones while the professor, Professor "Charlie" Brown, who Shar was convinced was suicidal, tried to get through his lecture. She texted me ongoing updates about Charlie Brown's mental state while I sat in a stadium of hundreds of future linguistic students trying to remember the difference between the types of verbs (which seemed to be key to understanding language).

Charlie Brown paler than usual.

CB cried thru lecture.

"Is his name really Charlie Brown?" I stupidly inquired after the first round of texts.

"It should be," Shar sneered. "GOOD GRIEF!"

Shar said there were people who made out at the back of the class and Charlie Brown just stood there behind his lectern and sulked.

By mid-October the idea of "classes" had begun to evaporate like steam from the sewer grates ascending into the rapidly cooling atmosphere. Shar pointed out that most of the lectures were available online or in the textbooks (which we still hadn't read), so what was the point of going to class?

Besides, there were so many more interesting ways to pass the time. We'd wake up and go for coffee. Then for breakfast. Then we'd watch a movie. Then to the park to smoke and watch other people who didn't have jobs or school as they walked around looking like idiots. Then sometimes we'd go to fancy office buildings and ask to see the "man in charge." Or we'd hang around until security asked us what we were doing there.

"Loitering," Shar would say.

We made time disappear. Or it just melted around us. We'd run out of things to do, then turn a corner and Shar would develop a new course of action.

"You know what we should do, Allison," she'd say, pulling me into or out of a cab.

"What?"

One day we spent the entire afternoon in a tattoo parlour pretending we were waiting for a friend to come get a tattoo.

"I dare you to talk to the first person who comes in," Shar whispered.

The first person was a scrawny woman wearing sweatpants with the words BOOTY SHAKE on the back. She had a sad face and long wavy hair that looked like brown seaweed.

As soon as she sat down Shar jabbed me, hard, in the side with her index finger.

"Here for a tattoo?" I asked, my voice cracking a little.

"Yeah," the woman said, holding up a picture of a horseshoe with a four-leaf clover on each side. "For my boyfriend Chuck."

"Wow," I said, "that's SO WEIRD because we're here ... uh ... waiting for OUR friend Chuck."

Shar nodded. "Chuck's going to get a memorial tattoo for his sister. What's he getting again? Do you remember, Allison?"

"He's getting his sister's name and ... uh."

"A toilet. Because she was bulimic."

"With her name engraved on the seat," I continued, suppressing a smile almost as cleanly as Shar, "or in toilet paper like a runner along the bottom."

"I didn't think you could die from that," Chuck's girlfriend gasped.

"OH. Yes," I said.

"People die from it every day," Shar whispered.

Outside, sunshine bounced off the plastic store signs. When I looked down, Shar and I were stride for stride as we rushed back to rez. Looking at her feet and mine in synch, I think that for a moment I actually forgot about things, things like the burns on my neck, Anne. Maybe not all of Anne, but most of her.

"I'm getting a memorial tattoo too," Shar said. "I'm going to get a toilet with your name on it."

"I'm going to get a picture of you upchucking," I added.

Shar thought that was pretty funny.

"Wow," she said, "that's hysterical, Allison."

When we were studying in her room Shar doodled on the covers of all her textbooks with a black Sharpie and then ripped them off and handed them to me. "Art for your otherwise boring and crappy room," she explained, flinging the ripped covers at me. "Keep them, Allison. Treasure them."

Semi-serious. An order but not an order. Like when

we'd go out and she'd say, "You know what we should do, Allison."

Of course, for the first little while hanging with Shar, in the back of my brain I had a nagging concern about not knowing what exactly her deal was. Part of me, because of my past, will always wonder what the deal is whenever anyone decides to be my friend, especially in cases where I can't see exactly what it is I'm bringing to the bargain.

Shar didn't seem to want anything from me, other than to have me follow her around.

Briefly, very briefly, I wondered if we'd eventually encounter the plot twist where it would be revealed that Shar was hanging out with me because she'd made a bet with her popular friends that she could earn my trust then break my heart, which is the twist in a shocking number of movies about teenagers.

Of course for that to be true, Shar would have to have some kind of posse of really popular friends, and Shar did not.

Actually, she didn't even seem to like a lot of people other than me.

One night we were lying around in her room drinking coffee and listening to her favourite old rock and roll, the Rolling Stones, when her floormates decided to have a RUNWAY WALK OFF in the hall.

Someone set up some speakers while the rest of the girls pushed the stacks of textbooks, mandarin peels, pop cans, and pizza boxes to the side. The first thing we heard was the pulse of bass. Then a squeal. When we opened the door, the scene in the corridor was like some sort of low-budget, modest Playboy mansion movie: girls were dancing in oversized T-shirts, frilly nighties, and pyjamas with the legs rolled up and waistbands rolled down. Some girls were even handing out spare heels for people to borrow. The Patties were there, with patent heels and surprisingly shapely calves. Mini Patty wasn't all that sturdy in pumps but she managed a nice plant and turn, pausing for a moment to pucker her lips, emphasizing her cheekbones, before she sashayed back down the brown carpet. Carly was there too, in a pink baby-doll nightie and pink heels, trotting down the hallway, light as air, the popcorn littering the hall barely crunching under her feet.

I fear dancing with the lights on in groups the way some people fear dark spaces at night. Next to the runway, I flattened myself against the wall as if someone was pressing me there, pushing the scarred part of my neck, which was suddenly insanely itchy, against the cool plaster. Out of the corner of my eye I watched as Shar stood stock-still and crossed her arms. Asian Patty spotted us and darted over to grab Shar by the elbow and pull her into the show.

"Walk it, Shar!" someone cheered as Asian Patty attempted to twirl her.

Shar was immovable. Her joints locked into place. A tiny sliver of what looked like the result of a bad smell pulsed across the surface of her face. As Asian Patty pulled, Shar put on an impossibly wide smile and backed away. "Uh. No."

"Oh come on!" someone behind us yelled. "Just let loose, Shar! Relax!"

Shar tugged her arm free with maybe a little more seriousness than anyone expected. The music stopped for a second while someone's iPod selected a new song. The pulse was slow to start up again.

Asian Patty let loose a little snort. "Uh. OKAY. I told you she wouldn't. What's your deal, party-pooper?"

Shar's smile tightened so that it looked like two parallel elastic bands stretched tight. "Hmmm. 'Party-pooper.' That's nice. What are you, seven?"

A sharp laugh erupted from my body. Asian Patty frowned. Shar grabbed my hand and pulled me back into her room.

"Whatever. What a bitch," Mini Patty coughed behind us.

Inside, Shar cranked the music and dropped back onto her bed. "You know what the best thing about college will be, Allison? Not even having to pretend to want to be a part of anyone else's stupid shit."

I was smiling. I could feel it on my face like one of those masks they paint on you at the circus or the fair, a big, wide, capital U in red and black.

A couple of days after the runway, Carly came to my room with an offering of Cultural Studies notes and a massive cellophane bag of pink popcorn.

"Hey! So, you haven't been … to class? So, I thought I'd bring you some notes and junk food."

"Holy crap, thanks. I'm oddly starving."

Dropping the bag on the bed, Carly tilted her head. "This used to be, like, my favourite food, so my mom sends me boxes."

"Not anymore?"

"Oh, I don't know. Maybe not." Carly twisted her mouth into a tiny frown for a second before adding, "I'm thinking I might not be so into pink now."

"So you can just switch your favourite colour, just like that?"

"Oh, you know, I'm pretty much always actively looking for a new favourite thing. I'm, like, serially non-monogamous when it comes to loving things. You know? I like liking lots of things. I like CHANGE, ya know? Like, when I was little, I NEVER wore skirts. Then one day I just decided. POOF. Into skirts. One day I hate pink. The next day, I'm a fricking bottle of Pepto-Bismol."

"Wow. That's kind of cool, I guess. I don't even have a favourite colour."

"You are SO FUNNY. How could you not have a favourite colour, Allison? You should get at least one." Carly smiled. "Let loose a little. Experiment."

Looking at the notes, I felt a tiny wave of guilt. "I'm totally coming to class next week by the way."

"Great. We should sit together." Turning to leave, Carly paused. "Did you …? Um. Do you know who broke the toaster oven downstairs?"

"What?"

"The toaster oven. Is broken."

"Oh. That sucks."

Carly was staring past me. The multitude of strange doodles had become an overwhelming presence in the space over my bed, and they fanned out behind me like a peacock's tail.

"But, uh, no," I finally added. "No, I mean, I don't know who did it."

"All right. I'm just asking around. Tori's really upset."

"How did it get broken? I mean, what happened?"

"Someone cut the power cord." Carly's little fingers, tips still painted pink, did a sad little snip.

"Wow. Wouldn't that … uh … wouldn't that electrocute you?"

"Um. Heh. No. Not if you unplugged it first?"

"Oh. Shit. Right. Duh. Fuck."

"Ha-ha-so. I guess it obviously wasn't you, huh?"

"Nope."

My phone went off with the weird ring Shar programmed, a maniacal laughing sound that cut into the space like a million X-Acto blades.

Carly did a quick spin and left my room.

That night, before she went to bed, Shar came upstairs and popped her head in the door. My room was dark so I couldn't see her face, just a silhouette leaning into my room, her voice in my ear.

"Hey, Allison?"

"Yeah."

"Nothing. I just wanted to say goodnight."

"Oh yeah, goodnight."

"Allison?"

"What?"

"I can't believe you've never played Truth or Dare."

"Yeah, sheltered I guess."

"Well, you're in college now. Lots of things to experience."

"I know, huh?"

"Okay, go to sleep. I'll see you tomorrow."

I listened to the sound of her footsteps as she disappeared down the hall. Soft taps on the carpet. Then the sound of Katy's white-noise machine, a last-ditch effort to conquer the morning's Metallica assault. The rhythmic *whooshing* of mechanical waves lulled me into, I'll admit, a pretty amazing sleep.

SIX

A.k.a.

Everyone has a name and something that people call them. What these things are, I think, has a pretty big impact on who you are.

Shar was named after her mother, Sharon, also named after her mother. Until Shar, I had no idea people actually did that, or still did that, to their kids. I thought it was something that only happened in tribes and medieval villages. Why, with the millions of names out there, would you name a kid after yourself?

"Is Sharon, like, a really old name?"

Chewing on a fistful of what was left of Carly's pink popcorn, pre-breakfast at Stack 'n' Flip, Shar shook her head. "It's the name of an old person."

Whenever Shar introduced herself or said her name to anyone, she made an obvious effort to make sure that whoever it was both knew her name and didn't call her Sharon. Very little pissed Shar off more than people calling her something she wasn't.

Which was funny.

Because, from what I could tell, Shar almost never called anyone by their real name.

First there were the Patties, a name that stuck even after the toaster oven thing. (A week later, the Patties purchased another toaster oven that they kept illegally in Asian Patty's room.)

Since the night of the film club meeting Carly was "Superstar."

The girl who lived in the room next to Shar, Natalie, was "Rattles" because she was always jumpy and nervous (and because her silent but constant piano practising next door rattled her bed against Shar's wall and drove her crazy).

Random people whose real names we never knew acquired tags after various incidents. Whatever the incident was, after Shar tagged them it was forever crystallized across their being. Like "Mr. Pickles," who may have been a really nice guy aside from the one time Shar caught him picking his nose then scraping the boogers on the underside of his seat. Then there was "Hives," the really tall, Shar thought gay, guy in our Social Problems class who always wanted to talk about HIV awareness and its impact on any and all social problems that came up in the lectures.

Not all the names were mean. There was "Notes," the guy who always gave Shar his notes for Enviro Geo. "Pam," Shar's other neighbour on her floor, had a legitimately nice pair of Pam Anderson–sized boobs and Shar didn't seem to hate her.

Shar never asked me who or what I was named after. I wasn't. My mom really wanted me to have a three-syllable name and my father had exes named Stephanie, Isabel, Jennifer, Gwendolyn, and Madeleine. So, my dad often noted, Allison was the obvious choice.

I've never actually had a nickname, although a lot of people in my life, mostly teachers, have called me Allie. Shar never called me anything but Allison, and she called me Allison often, the punctuation that bracketed our conversations.

"Right, Allison?"

Until Halloween, of course, when I stopped being just Allison and started, from time to time, being Sonny.

Sonny and Shar.

Get it?

Because we were Sonny and Cher for Halloween that year?

Clearly it was more complicated than that.

Beyond my name, I was pretty sure of a bunch of things before Halloween. I was sure Shar didn't sleep with girls, because she'd mentioned a couple boyfriends. I was pretty sure she thought I didn't sleep with girls either, because when people think you're not straight, especially girls, they usually want to ask you a bunch of totally inappropriate and stupid questions.

I was also, on a different level, pretty sure that Shar and I weren't going to be doing anything specific for Halloween, especially not any shindig put on by the college. Shar had an intense reaction to every -fest and -a-thon St. Joseph's had thrown thus far, which included the BBQ-fest, the Rap-fest, the (vaguely titled) Culture-a-thon, and the unpopular Fitness-a-thon. The only positive side to any of these events was that they left the TV room free for our personal TV-and-junk-food-fests.

It wasn't until Carly brought it up at breakfast the morning of, in the buzz of the early cafeteria rush, that Shar expressed any interest in Halloween festivities.

"Hey! Everyone's dressing up and coming to the dance, right?"

Shar raised an eyebrow. "What are 'us' dressing up as?"

"Uh. Well." Carly huffed and turned to face Shar, squaring her shoulders. "WE, as in a bunch of us, are all going as *Grease*. The movie? From Cultural Studies? Were you there for that class? Allison?"

I wasn't, but I'd seen the movie. My dad's company had had a *Grease* party once. "Right. Oh, so like with the pink ladies? Are you going as a pink lady?" I asked, easily picturing Carly in a pink silk jacket.

"No way! Are you kidding? I'm going as Danny Zuko! You know, the greaser? I loooooove John Travolta." Carly curled her lip and did some hunky shoulder moves. "But you guys can come and be pink ladies."

"Nope!" Shar cut in, before I had a chance to respond. "We've got plans."

"We do?"

"Yes, Allison, we do."

I still have no idea where Shar found costumes. She skipped Enviro Geology and then somehow, by dinner, she returned with a set of faux Native American disco suits, which she laid out on her bed on top of a pile of dirty black laundry.

"Check it out! Sonny and Cher!"

They were polyester, bedazzled with sequins and trimmed with feathers. The back of the Cher outfit was covered with gold-stitched dreamcatchers and little horses.

"Holy shit that's so cool."

"Fuck PINK LADIES. Like we're going as the fucking pink ladies."

Shar smiled. The muscles in her face softened, relaxed.

"I'm going to dress you up and everything," she said. "It's going to be amazing."

I'd never had anyone dress me up. It's a strangely comforting sensation, having someone else be in charge of what you're going to look like.

First Shar sent me into the bathroom with a tensor bandage and my smallest jogging bra so I could bind my boobs up. Then we fitted me into the jumpsuit, which required a bunch of safety pins and tape. Shar even borrowed some platform boots from Rattles—a stretch because Shar disliked Rattles—so that the cuffs wouldn't drag too much on the ground. My wig scratched my burn scar a bit so we added a little red handkerchief that I went and grabbed from Carly. The consensus was that I looked like a discount Sonny Bono.

"It's okay," Shar said. "I'm going to look really good as Cher."

By nine, the whole residence was like backstage at Radio City Music Hall, with girls running in and out of rooms borrowing makeup, jewellery, and fishnets. The tops of all the sinks were dusted with eye shadow and sticky with hairspray. Music bumped through the corridors as, cloistered in Shar's room, I watched her apply a layer of thick eyeliner, her long black wig glistening unnaturally like an oil spill running down her back.

It's not surprising that Shar looked really cool as Cher. So I won't go into it. But she looked amazing. Like long and lean and sparkly and regal, the way Cher looks in all her videos except in the one where she's wearing a weird leather bathing suit.

In the elevator down, after a few beers and a shot in her room, Shar/Cher hooked her arm around me and, with a slight, Cher-like drawl, crooned, "Sonny. Babe. What do you say you and me hit the town?" She smelled like hairspray, which was oddly intoxicating.

A set of *Dreamgirls*, in matching sparkly blue dresses, black gloves, and Afro wigs, pressed into the elevator, giggling.

"Cher. Honey," I replied, with a fairly un–Sonny Bono somewhat British accent, "I'd, uh, love to get groovy with you tonight."

"This is going to work better if you don't talk so much, Allison."

"Right."

Surprisingly, college dances are not all that different from high school dances. The Student Union building was done up in typical Halloween paper cut-outs, and plastic jack-o'-lanterns and mummies had been Scotch-taped onto every surface, making it hard to find someplace to lean. The theme was sort of a "dance" type thing and so someone had somehow hung a whole bunch of disco balls from the ceiling. Little orange and green lights flickered around the room like cat toys as the space started to fill up with costumes. There were zombies and Goths (who probably weren't even really dressed up) scattered everywhere. The engineers who came (including Hope) were all woodland animals (which seemed to entail a lot of humping demonstrations). A couple drag queens circled the room in glittery dresses and tall patent-leather boots, looking like glamorous storm troopers. A bunch of guys came dressed as condoms (not really ideal for picking up a date, but I guess it sent the right message). Carly and a bunch of people, including what looked like some of the guys from the film society, were the entire cast of *Grease*.

It's not strange that things got a little weird and messy that night. Although how and why they got messy the way they did was a surprise. At some point Shar and I were just awkwardly standing in the doorway. Then someone got us some beer. Then we posed with the Village People. Then we posed with the cast of *Grease*. Then Shar/Cher and I posed for someone working for the newspaper who wanted a picture of us "as a couple."

Shar/Cher grinned. "Ya gonna kiss me, Sonny?"

I think I grinned back. "You wanna kiss, uh, Cher?"

I remember leaning in and thinking, Fake kiss. No big deal. Fake kiss.

I was surgically careful. Edged closer in a series of degrees.

As our lips met, like someone touching a new baby's forehead, behind us I could hear whoops and hollers.

"Sonny. That's the way you kiss your wife?" Shar smirked as we headed to the bar.

"What do you mean?"

"What do you think?"

Shar/Cher spun around, pressed her finger on my already damp moustache.

Briefly, time stopped. Shar/Cher's face came so close to mine I could see the ring of perspiration forming along the coastline where her wig dug into her forehead. Her breath smelled like gum. But she wasn't chewing gum. Her eyes looked different, less calm, less collected, like there was suddenly something happening behind the layer of her irises.

I couldn't say what.

"There's nothing wrong with it, Sonny."

"What? Yeah. I mean, I know."

You can make a person's heart beat faster for a multitude of reasons, medical, social, sociopathic. What kind of person makes another person's heart beat faster just for kicks?

And then disappears?

Cher/Shar was drinking shots at the bar with the rest of *Grease* and some vaguely familiar girls dressed up like Playboy bunnies, and then she was gone.

It took me three songs to realize she wasn't coming back. Not any time soon anyway.

I guess I had no right to be pissed off, but I totally was.

Using my (still unreturned) Jennifer Taylor ID, I ordered another drink. Then I went and sat in the corner with a bunch of stoned-looking dudes who weren't in costume, where I was approached by a tall dude in black, wearing a pumpkin head and a top hat. A tall dude who appeared somewhat magically out of a disco smoke while the Cure was playing.

"Greetings and salummmfph." The pumpkin bowed awkwardly, holding his head up so as not to pitch forward and, presumably, lose his hat. His voice was a muffled chirp hidden within layers of what looked like real pumpkin. "May I mmmmphf as to the mmmphf of your seventies atmmph?"

"What?"

Removing the head and replacing the top hat, the familiar boy smiled and sat.

"Uh. Yes. I was saying, uh, greetings and salutations. You're in my Social Problems class, I believe. I was asking about your, uh, funky seventies outfit. I was, uh, attempting some random college dance small talk as it were."

"I'm supposed to be Sonny. From Sonny and Cher."

"Ah yes. 'I Got You Babe.' Excellent. Allow me to introduce myself. I am Jonathon." Dude looked more nervous and out of place than anyone I'd met since arriving at St. Joseph's, which was both thrilling (because it wasn't me) and super annoying (because other people's nervousness, unless they're good looking, is annoying).

Jonathon, nervous or not, blabbed on in a stream of weirdly accented talk. "It is a pleasure to make your acquaintance. I suppose I am 'Pumpkin Head' for the purposes of this particular event."

Disco light danced in the crevices of Jonathon's pitted skin. Looking at him, I had a moment of memory, a burp of recognition. Social Problems class. RIGHT! This was the guy who'd tripped the basketball player in the hallway the first day of class. An underwhelming St. Joseph's legend sitting next to me.

Big hairy deal.

"Right."

"And you? Your name is?"

"OH. Right. I'm Allison," I blurted, scanning the room for the non-existent Shar.

"Pretty interesting spectrum, wouldn't you say?" Jonathon remarked, following my gaze around the room. "A little bit of nostalgia, a little bit of pop culture minutiae. Possibly a few too many boys dressed as serial killer–type creatures for anyone's comfort. I believe there's a Paris Hilton by the bar. And there's about three fellows dressed as Harry Potter, no surprise."

"Sure, whatever."

"Feels eerily close to every high school dance you ever went to, though, does it not?" Jonathon tilted his pumpkin head up to peer into its empty triangle eyes. "Although of course every nerd here is praying it's not ... high school."

"Sure," I said again. Who was this dude talking to, anyway? Me, a.k.a. the OTHER nerd in the room?

A lumberjack ambled over and leaned in my general direction. "HEY! Are you a GIRL?"

"Yes," I grumbled.

"Can I get you a beer?"

"No."

I had a sudden urge to either close my eyes or cry.

Leaning over, Jonathon sighed. "It's not that bad is it?"

"What?"

"Oh. Nothing. Ah. Are you entirely opposed to the notion of a pint with a stranger? I thought perchance I might offer us up some libation."

"Uh. I gotta go." The night was shitty enough without having to spend it listening to a pumpkin head rambling on in Middle English.

I headed over to the bar and had another drink.

Walked around the room, weaving in and out of groups of people standing and shouting at each other.

My wig was itchy and sweat was starting to trickle down my neck a bit, little rivers of salt running across the tender surface of past injuries.

FUCK Halloween.

More beer.

My seventh round at the bar I spotted Shar/Cher on the dance floor. A bunch of guys dressed as cowboys pinged her back and forth between them like a pinball machine.

Technically, I mumbled to myself, I could just leave. Shar was a big girl who could get home on her own. Cher, of course, had a long and fruitful career without Sonny.

But then Shar/Cher returned as suddenly as she'd left. She crept up behind me and wrapped her arms around my waist. Leaned into me and put her chin on my good shoulder. "You're watching me," she blurted into my ear.

"Um. NO," I said, spinning around, "I'm not watching you. Where have you been?"

Shar pressed forward, heavy lips curved up into a grin, eyes bent under the weight of plastic lashes.

"You're WATCHING ME. ALWAYS. Right? You like WATCHING me?"

My body buzzed with alcohol. When I run, sometimes the feeling of having my feet move so fast when my head feels so still makes me dizzy.

This sensation was not dissimilar.

"I'm just here with you," I said aloud.

"What?"

"I SAID, I'M JUST—"

"Hey!" It was Carly in her little leather jacket and jeans, looking very much like a tiny Travolta and very much unlike herself.

"What can we do for you, Superstar?" Shar slurred, gripping my arm even tighter.

"I think we're going to the other party!" Carly shouted at me, ignoring Shar.

"WHAT?"

"Are you guys COMING?"

"NO!" Shar screamed, leaning forward, almost toppling Carly over. "We're STAYING because THIS party is the BEST!"

The B-52s came on and there was a rush. Shar pulled

my arm and backed into the crowd, all the while shouting at Carly, "BYE, SUPERSTAR!"

Bodies pogoed around us. It was like being an egg in a pot of boiling water.

"You want to dance with me, RIGHT? RIGHT Sonny?" Shar's eyes were completely dilated. Hard dark circles that jittered with the music.

"Okay!"

Dropping her body weight onto me, Shar/Cher planted her face by my ear. "I have to tell you something."

"What?"

Pulling back, she yanked me out the other side of the dancing crowd. "Come here."

They say that when a person looks at your lips it means they're about to kiss you. Unless the person is a dentist. As far as I know, this is true. The first time I kissed Anne I'd been staring at her lips for hours, sitting on the couch next to her while we watched soaps. I remember reaching forward and touching Anne's knee, feeling the tiny prickles of the spots she'd missed shaving. First kiss. Body shaking.

With glittery dance lights swooping overhead, I watched Shar/Cher's eyes shift down to my moustache. Watched her eyelashes with the tiny rhinestones on the rim twinkle as her weight shifted forward, into my arms, and her lips pressed against mine.

"WAIT!" something inside me screamed. But then Shar/Cher's fingers pushed into my back and whatever ideas I had for self-preservation floated up into the rafters like so many soap bubbles, popping against the bass of the music while a little piece of me slipped out of my mouth, into hers.

Shar's kiss was ravenous and overwhelming. Her arms wrapped around me, pulling me tighter.

"Let's go, Sonny," she mumbled, her breath pushing against mine. "Let's get out of here before I change my mind."

We ended up messing around in my bed, mostly kissing. I think. I tried to focus and steady myself but my brain was awash with lips and alcohol. At some point Shar's nail dragged across my burn, cat-claw hard, and I cried out. I remember my head hitting the wall and Shar's dress ripping. I remember wishing I knew how to do something other than kiss and grab at her.

Of course, if I'd known this was in any way possible, I would have done some sort of preparation. As someone who'd only really done anything with one person, I was pretty aware of the fact that my skills were kind of lacking in terms of sexy moves. I won't go into details, but for those of you who think girls who sleep with girls have it any better because they're more familiar with the equipment, let me just say, that's fucking stupid. It's like saying having hair makes you a hairdresser or having a body makes you a masseuse.

In the dark, in a fog of booze, I tried to distinguish the outline of Shar's eyes from the complex of shadows on her face. I couldn't help feeling illuminated in the light of the moon outside. Fully clothed, tragically, and yet oddly exposed. Eventually I closed my eyes. My lips went numb. I forgot who I was holding.

I don't remember falling asleep, but when I woke up, Shar was gone, her wig a limp tarantula on the pillow.

SEVEN

Sex is a problem

The day after Halloween, I rolled out of bed and into the bathroom where I barfed. Violently. Several times. After a period of recuperation, a swig out of a pop bottle of mystery brown fizzy contents, and a shower, I managed to collect myself and find my way to Social Problems.

One twenty-five p.m. Time for my "morning" class.

I was late, and fumbled my way into a seat as Professor J paused to take a couple of chugs from her giant bottle of green Gatorade. The auditorium was a mass of hungover students, clearly unable to sit up unaided. The seats closest to the walls were in high demand. I caught sight of top hat, a.k.a. Pumpkin Head, a.k.a. Jonathon waving at me from his perch in the top row.

I wondered if he smelled like pumpkin. I immediately stopped wondering when it became clear that thinking about food made my stomach want to turn itself inside out.

"The question we must ask ourselves, of course," Professor J was saying, "is whether we as a society even *know* we have a problem. Or, better yet, *how* we know when something is a problem."

In the seats next to me, two girls were doodling back and forth on a notebook. One girl drew a sperm and the other started making a jacking-off motion in her lap.

"You're going to say, 'There are symptoms.' Of course there are. How do we know we have an economic problem? We have symptoms. We have a rise in unemployment. Debt. But what else? How else do we know we have a problem?"

College professors ask a lot of questions they don't want answered. I'd had no idea what a rhetorical question even was until after a couple of weeks at college when I went back to my room and out of boredom searched "questions you don't answer" on Google.

I got a page about talking to kids about sex and a page on "rhetorical" questions. Rhetorical questions sound like questions but they're not. They're leads people use for talking about something they want to talk about.

On the screen behind the podium, a series of posters flashed. Propaganda. Pictures of kids smoking pot with the word "MARIJUANA" in big monster-green letters. World War II posters of the "ORIENTAL MENACE." A pamphlet about promiscuity with a girl sitting in a doctor's office weeping.

"We know we have a problem because people tell us we have a problem. Not always so bluntly. It's not every day that someone comes up to you on the street and TELLS you that you have a problem. No. Society tells us we have a problem in other ways."

I wrote down in my notes, *How know if have problem?* And then promptly scratched it out because it seemed like the stupidest thing ever written.

Especially on that particular day.

"Sex is a good thing to talk about with regard to this phenomenon," Professor J noted. "And when I say sex is a problem I'm not saying what you think I'm saying."

Baffled-slash-hungover silence.

"That was a joke."

More silence.

No one ever laughed at Professor J's jokes. Ever. Listening to her tell jokes reminded me of being in grade five. My parents had given me a subscription to *Jokes, Jokes, Jokes* magazine with the idea that it might make me loosen up and/or gain more friends at school. All it did was give people the impression that I was insane. A chronic teller of unfunny jokes. To this day whenever anyone utters the phrase "Knock, knock" I get queasy.

Professor J was not unfunny. I sometimes thought about catching her in the hall and saying, You know, I think you're funnier than that class would indicate. Although I had the impression she didn't give a shit whether people thought she was funny. I was also pretty sure that if I was to approach her anywhere outside that classroom she'd have no idea who I was.

At that point, I hadn't seen Shar all day. She wasn't in class and hadn't called me and I basically hadn't called her either, given that I was totally freaked out. Because?

Because sex with people who are your "friends" messes things up. Sex with girls, especially, messes everything up.

That's not what Professor J's lecture was about, but that's what I was thinking that afternoon: sex with girls. Sex with girls, I thought. Problem?

Which is a question I should have known the answer to by then.

Like, take Anne for example.

About a week after Anne and I slept together, which happened a little after Christmas break, she told me she'd realized that the whole thing was a horrible accident and that she was really upset about it. This conversation will always stick out in my brain as one of the worst verbal exchanges I've ever had. Even better, it happened on the PHONE. January 15. At Starbucks. Like, four o'clock in the aft, I was getting a hot chocolate and I had her on the phone, crying, while I was paying. She was crying so loud that the girl giving me my change actually stopped and tried to listen in.

"JESUS CHRIST I'm not a LESBIAN. JESUS you didn't tell anyone I'm a lesbian, did you?"

"No."

"Did y—" There was a series of choking and sobbing sounds.

The barista smiled a weak smile, leaning so far forward she could have grabbed a sip from my hot chocolate.

"WHAT? Did I what?"

"Tell anyone about—THE THING?"

"What thing?"

"THE THING! The *thing* we *did*."

More sobbing.

Messed up.

I spent an hour sitting on the curb next to my quickly cooling beverage, talking Anne down, reassuring her that everything was cool. That what had happened between us was not only a distant memory but a non-issue. Like, it never happened. I was erasing it from history as we spoke. Every word felt like chewing on a dirty caramel, hard against my teeth and throat.

"It's okay. Anne. It was just like, a little mistake. Seriously."

After that phone call, Anne was only, like, grudgingly my friend. She'd invite me to things and then cancel. In March, she got a boyfriend and texted me a message.

I have a BF now. So you know.

Then she didn't speak to me at all.

Which is to say that after the St. Joseph's Halloween party I basically tied my stomach in a knot and hated myself all day for having been a stupid asshole. Of course, I thought, I've done it again. I've royally messed up AGAIN and now I'm just as screwed. AGAIN.

And then. And then, that night, Shar just sort of showed up at my door. She looked like how she always looked. Not nervous or weirded out or anything. She said she wanted to go find hair bleach.

"So are you coming or what, Allison?"

"Uh, coming. Yeah, okay, let's go."

It wasn't until later, sitting in the bathroom on Shar's floor with her hair all wrapped in Saran Wrap in a chemical soup, that she finally turned to me and said, "How long have you been gay?"

"What?"

"You're a lesbian, right? Or. Are you bi?"

I'm not really sure what bi is, to be honest. Like, to me it sounds as if you know you'll sleep with the same number of boys as girls. But how would you even know that? Does it mean you have to sleep with a boy after you do it with a girl? What if all the boys in your town are stupid?

"I guess I'm a, uh, into girls."

"Do you have a girlfriend?"

I must have looked stunned.

"You have a girlfriend?! You just cheated on your girlfriend." Tapping the plastic wrap to check for heat, Shar looked suddenly satisfied.

"Yeah. NO. I didn't. I don't. I mean, I had this girl I went out with for a while in high school."

"Ooooo, Allison! High school girlfriend." Shar grinned. "You break up with her?"

I pictured Anne sitting in a huddle with her other friends while I sat in my little homosexual seat. OutCAST. Why would anyone want to reveal that experience? Like, yeah, I slept with this girl and she instantly regretted it and then decided she hated me. And then I totally flipped out and couldn't talk to anyone, which was fine because by then I was a complete social pariah. Now I'm here.

I had a brief thought that somehow, if I told Shar about it, she might do the same thing.

Like, hate me.

Everyone knows that people hate/dump people who get dumped all the time. I have this feeling that it's easier to dump someone you know someone else has dumped. It's like throwing out something you bought at a garage sale.

The other side of the lie being, of course, that I didn't want to be that desperate lesbian dumped by a clearly non-lesbian anymore. And lying was the easiest way to make that true. In, okay, a very superficial way.

"Yeah, well," I sighed, "you know how it goes. I'm not really a commitment person."

"Ha. You fucker. You're all, 'See ya!'"

Outside, Shar's floormates were screaming the lyrics of a pop tune I didn't recognize. It was nine p.m., and they'd just come off of watching their weird singing sitcom. Sitcoms made Shar's floormates crazy.

"Your floormates are weird."

"Allison. My floormates are neanderthals. Some idiot THREW UP in the hallway last night. Little upchucked candy corn and Bailey's right outside the bathroom. How high school is that? Do you understand what I'm saying? It's too much trouble to walk two steps and barf in the sink like everyone else?"

"Totally."

"If I knew who it was I'd barf on HER door, see what she thought of that. I think it was Asian Patty."

Shar turned and looked in the mirror, then stroked the underside of her chin with her finger. "I'm not into girls, but I mess around with them sometimes."

"Oh, yeah?"

"I probably should have told you that, but I figured you were gay so you wouldn't care."

"Oh. Right. Sure."

"It's because I think they're safe, you know? Girls. After having so many messed-up boys in my life. It's like, I know that girls won't turn crazy on me or mess with me. Also. I had a boy in my life who was very fucked up. Like, abusive. He used to, you know, hit me."

"Fuck. Shar. I'm so sorry."

"It totally wrecked me up for a while." She stopped for a moment to stare at her reflection, like she was looking for something, checking for something. "But I'm over it now."

"Wow."

"Yeah." Shar turned from the mirror to look at me. Whatever she saw on my face made a tiny smile feather into the corners of her lips. "I'm so glad I can tell you this shit, Allison. Seriously. I'm so glad you're here. I would shoot myself in the face if you weren't here."

"Same."

It took a while to rinse all the bleach out of Shar's hair, but when we were finished her already blond hair was, like, translucent. It made her look like a ghost.

When she disappeared to get her hair dryer I took a long look in the mirror. I'd probably never had as many mirrors in my life as I did in that dorm. Everywhere you looked there you were, reflected in the walls, looking back. I've pretty much always hated looking at myself in the mirror. I look weird. Like, even though I'm seventeen, I have grey hairs. Not a ton but enough. I'm like a faded version of a person, really. Even my clothes, because I washed them in the crappy dorm machines, were faded: black T-shirts gone grey, dark jeans, light blue. I wondered how Shar could even believe I'd had a girlfriend, let alone dumped one.

My burn, which had stopped hurting on any regular basis, was seared and sore today where Shar's fingernail had made contact. A sharp red line dissected its shiny, slightly puckered layer of new skin.

"I need to fix my hair," I said when she returned with a fistful of hair product.

"Yeah. You should go black," Shar mused, rubbing a drop of product into the fragile ends of her bangs. "You look a bit washed out."

"Oh. Really?"

"Yeah. And maybe sometime you could borrow some of my clothes. My black jeans would look good on you."

"Really?"

Shar shrugged. "Why not?"

Outside the door there was a thump, followed by a whimper. We peered out of the bathroom to find Rattles in the hallway, lying on the carpet, clinging to her cell phone.

When I walked up to her she rolled over into a fetal position.

"Are you okay?" I asked, bending down on one knee.

Rattles turned her head and pushed her face into the carpet, possibly breathing in small particles of leftover barf.

"Noooooooooo," she moaned. Her body, appropriately, rattled with sobs.

"Allison. ALLISON." Shar stood by her room. "I'm starving. Let's get out of here."

"She's upset," I mouthed, one hand tentatively placed on Rattles's shaking shoulder.

Shar frowned, pushed the door open, and disappeared into her room.

"Rat— Natalie?" I whispered. "What happened?"

I had no idea what to do. She clearly didn't have any bleeding wounds.

Just then Rattles let out a howling sob from the bottom of her lungs. Which is about when Asian Patty cracked open her door.

"What's WRONG?" she cried. "NAT! HEY, GUYS!"

Asian Patty's cry was enough to alert the whole floor. Pretty soon a small mob had gathered around Rattles, squeezing me out of the immediate circle of assistance. Carly arrived from out of nowhere and was soon wedged under Rattles's sobbing frame.

Someone I didn't recognize pressed her ear close to Rattles's face, like you'd press your ear against a train track. "Oh my gosh, her boyfriend broke up with her," she whispered. "On the PHONE."

"NO!"

"SHIT."

"Oh Nat. I'm so sorry. It's going to be okay."

"I'm ordering pizza," someone in the back piped in.

"I'm getting beer."

"Oh I have some booze left."

"I have chocolate!"

"Someone get ice cream!"

A potluck. Actually, these group get-togethers over boyfriend breakups had been springing up with increasing frequency since September. By November, more than half the girls who'd arrived with boyfriends were single/slutty.

"Is she going to be all right?" I asked Carly, for no reason other than the fact that she seemed to be at that moment the most physically bonded to Rattles.

"It'll be okay." Carly smiled. "Right, Natalie? This boyfriend stuff sucks but it will pass."

Eventually Shar reappeared from her room and tapped me, hard, on the shoulder.

"She's not DYING, Allison, and she's got the whole ER now. Can we go?"

In the elevator, Shar scratched at a heart that someone had carved in the faux wood finish of the wall. "Those girls are so fucking pathetic it kills me. You know, the more you pay attention to someone like that, the worse they get."

That night, to celebrate her new hair, we went to THE KEGGER, a fraternity fav hangout, and spent the whole night vying to see who could get away with stealing more beers from drunken boys. Extra points were awarded for whole pitchers. It wasn't really much of a contest. I was too timid. Shar stretched out an early lead. She swiped beers directly from frat boys' sweaty palms, distracting them with a smile and a flash of platinum blonde. Every stolen drink was followed by a hysterical victory lap on the dance floor, which became increasingly jubilant as more beers were successfully snatched.

"Uh, we're drinking traces of boy spit with every pint," I noted.

"Fuck it." Shar grinned. "Maybe we can go out and sexually assault some innocent girl after this. Break some girl's heart in two with our bare hands."

By the sixth drink we were pouring pints into each other's mouths as the jocks danced around us in their ugly outfits, vying for Shar's attention and not getting it.

We moshed until I couldn't see straight, twirling each other into a blur. We danced until the blitz of stolen beers and sweatshirts enveloped me.

Then we stumbled home.

"THIS GIRL," Shar screamed at every passerby between the bar and the dorm, "IS THE FUCKING BEST. SHE IS A FUCKING MONSTER AND A

HEARTBREAKER. YOU DO NOT WANT TO GET IN
HER WAY."

When we got back to the dorm, girls were still sitting
in the hallway, listening to sad songs and sucking on
the last of the popped popcorn kernels. There was
a girl on either side of Rattles, who was slumped by
her door, her phone clenched in her hand.

The whole incident put Shar in the appetite for
watching *The Sopranos*. Which we did. Until
four a.m.

EIGHT

Perished-ables

The theory of evolution, as I've always understood it at least, says that creatures need to adapt to their environments … in order to survive. So, it's either adapt or, you know, "perish," which is a nice way of saying "die," although it's also, confusingly, a term my mom used to use for dairy products that had gone bad.

Perished-ables.

To "adapt" to college life can mean a number of things. For some people it's adapting to the schedule, which is not really all that different from high school's if you go to classes. Other people talk about adapting to the party life, to drinking and staying up late. Technically this is a matter of building up your tolerance. Although from what I saw, the puke patches became more frequent, not less, as the months got on.

Really, adaptation is change that you eventually become used to or okay with. It's change that's not accompanied by a meltdown.

Some things can adapt. Like people—okay, *most* people. There are other things that can't adapt. Like fish. Fish are pretty much screwed if you try to make them adapt. I know this as someone who has killed the odd goldfish. You can't even mess with the temperature of their water. They will die on you. Truth.

People not adapting at college seemed to experience similarly drastic consequences. The boyfriend breakup thing is a good example of typical college freshman freak-outage.

There was a mix of responses to the breakup. Girls who'd once stayed home waiting for phone calls started going out and getting wasted and then loudly calling their (ex-)boyfriends when they returned. One girl, in the room right above mine, broke up with her boyfriend on the phone and then threw her cell out the window. It hit some guy's car parked on the street and cracked the windshield. Which is a $2000 fine.

Whoops.

Boyfriends weren't the only reason people freaked out at college. Overall, as it got colder and people got more and more into college life, it sort of seemed like there was a growing number of students going a bit nutso. It was as though everyone had been playing the same video game for too long, eyes all fringed with thin red lines.

Foreshadowing these meltdowns, around the end of November, posters showed up all over campus with the message, "ANXIOUS? We're here to help!" The poster had information about a college-run website and a bunch of little tags with the address on them. Like those LOST DOG PLEASE CALL posters with the phone numbers. It wasn't long before those little tabs started to get ripped off a lot. You'd see them peeking out of the tops of people's textbooks and wallets. Like a little ANXIOUS flag.

The whole thing reached a noticeable decibel around the end of term when suddenly everyone had to hand in papers and study for exams, which, I have to say, just sort of suddenly HAPPENED. One day Shar and I were in Cultural Studies for the screening of a movie Carly had warned me wasn't available anywhere else, and I noticed a date written on the front board.

"Holy shit, is that our EXAM?"

Several students nodded. Several more rolled their eyes.

"What is that, next week?"

"Two weeks," Carly, who was sitting a row behind and two seats over, mumbled, looking at me the way a person looks at a stupid younger brother.

The next obvious question being what, other than the movie we were about to watch, would be on that exam.

"Ask Superstar for her notes," Shar suggested, wadding up a ball of gum in her fingers and planting it under her seat. "Wait, why are we seeing this movie?"

Of course I was an arts student, a group that's almost expected, from what I understood, to screw off on their exams. I heard this one story about a guy who didn't study or go to class for any of his courses because he wanted to see if he could pass without doing any of those things. He failed, but, you know, at least it wasn't a wasted effort. The other story I heard in the caf was about a guy who'd just Wikipedia'd the key words from the titles of all his courses the day before exams. But by the time I heard that rumour the dude was a second-year student, so, you know, he must have passed something.

The people who were truly, and rightly, tearing their hair out were the science students who had real exams that were, I heard, super difficult. Hope, the engineering student on my floor, abruptly stopped drinking alcohol at the end of November and started chugging energy-boost drinks. She hated her room and so more often than not she studied in the bathroom, throwing dirty looks at anyone who went in to use the space for ... well, what you'd normally use a bathroom for. Eventually the whole floor got sick of fighting with her and we all started showering and peeing and everything else on the next floor up.

My plan for exams, once I realized they were happening, was really an adaptation of Shar's, cooked up over late-late-night pizza and *The Shining* in the common room. Basically, I would read everything I could find, beg, borrow, or steal that related to the course. And in reading I would hope that SOMETHING would lodge itself in my brain. Hopefully something useful, like a date or the name of a dictator or a fact.

"Your brain is stickier than you think," Shar reasoned, pressing her pizza-smudgy finger into my forehead. "All you really need to do is read everything once. It's not like you're becoming an expert or anything. You're a FRESHman."

Which is how it happened that, on the night of Rattles's accident, Shar and I were in her room reading. Truthfully what I was doing would probably be better described as "looking," staring at the pages of my textbook in sequence, while Shar watched videos on the internet of people drowning. We almost didn't hear Rattles over the cries of the tidal-wave victims floating across Shar's screen.

Rattles, since her tragic breakup, had not quite embraced the single lifestyle. If anything she seemed to have given up the notion of any kind of lifestyle at all. She'd gone from preppy chic to a wardrobe of utter indifference, wearing the same giant college sweatshirt and baggy-kneed yoga pants. Her hair was always tied up in a loose ponytail that appeared to be, kind of tellingly, unravelling. At night she would wander the halls of the dorm, aimlessly peeking into various rooms to say hi to whoever was awake.

"Hi. Um. Hey. Um. What are you doing?"

If you were eating she'd pick at your food. If you were reading she'd interrupt your reading to ask you what you were reading. If you were watching TV she'd perch somewhere on the side, expel deep sighs, and ask questions like "So what's going on? Is that guy dead? Is this a history movie? Are you guys finding this hard to follow?" All in the same squeaky, sad-sounding voice. Eventually she'd sigh and move on, like an animal in the zoo that's tired of looking at you through the fence and so retreats to its cave.

At some point she'd duck out to a convenience store and return with massive bags of salt and vinegar chips and big bottles of Coke, which she was reluctant to share.

"Oh you want some? Um, yeah. I guess. But, um, this is kind of all I can eat now?"

Rattles was in the music program, and so at least half of her exams involved playing really long and really hard piano pieces. From her constant whimpering, just about everyone in the dorm knew she'd had a lot of trouble practising since her boyfriend broke up with her, which was causing her, to say the least, a lot of stress.

As soon as I noticed the sound of crying that night I knew it had to be Rattles. When I opened the door to see what was going on, she was on her hands and knees on the hallway carpet picking pills up off the floor. Her pale face looked even paler under the fluorescent hall lights.

"I spilled my pills," she sobbed.

"Oh," I said, hoping the pills were at least over-the-counter medication.

"Where is everyone?" Rattles looked up, her eyes pressed into her skull.

"I think they're all at the library or something."

"They've all gone to see a movie," Shar hollered from behind me.

"Oh yeah. I guess you guys didn't want to see a movie?" Rising from the carpet, not unlike some sort of creepy flickering Japanese horror film character, Rattles slowly shifted toward me. Her track pants were too long and the cuffs scraped against the carpet the way little kids' pyjamas do.

"You guuuys," she whined as she brushed past me, zombie-like, "I don't know what I'm going to DOOO!"

Three steps into Shar's room, she sunk down to the floor. "I have an exam tomorrow!? But I CAN'T take it, you know? I just CAN'T. It's like ... It's like OH MY GOD, you know?" Tears dribbled down her cheeks. "I'm so stressed out."

Shar snapped her laptop shut and moved to sit on the bed. I sort of thought she would ask Rattles to leave.

Looking at the pills in her palm, Rattles sighed. "It's like, I wish maybe I had some sort of massive injury, you know? Like, can they make you take an exam if you have a broken leg or like a torn tibia?"

"Well," I reasoned, "probably not an exam where you need your feet. Don't pianos need feet? Or, like, involve you using your foot?"

Shar shifted. Looked at me. Looked at Rattles. She lit a cigarette and opened the window a crack. "Obviously. Obviously they won't make you take an exam with a broken leg. You'd be in the hospital."

She took a long drag off her smoke. Exhaled. Then, checking on Rattles again, she said, "I think they have to let you out of an exam if you're unfit to write—"

"Oh my GOD I'm TOTALLY unfit to do ANYTHING right now!" Rattles sobbed. "I, like, can't sleep. I'm sad all the time. I'm like DEPRESSED, you know? It's like, FUCK! I'm like EATING all the time—"

"Yeah, yeah," Shar cut in. "Except they can't just go letting people who are depressed get a free pass for feeling sad. No offence, but lots of people feel sad. What I'm saying is that you'd need to be PHYSICALLY unfit to get out of an exam."

"Oh," Rattles moaned, threading her fingers into her hair and pulling. "UGH! Whatever. It's HOPELESS. I'm going to fail!"

"Sure." Shar nodded. Her voice had taken on a weird rhythm—like something almost robotic, but soothing, steady, and deliberate. "Or. Maybe. Maybe you COULD find some way out of it. It's like you said, if you were INJURED you couldn't play, right?"

"What?" Rattles's voice seemed to be breaking up into smaller and smaller pieces with every word she spoke.

"If you were injured. You couldn't play. So?"

Rattles bent her head and started to cry again, the kind of crying that seems more to do with exhaustion than anything really sad. A tear dripped off her cheek and onto the floor. Watching it splash against the linoleum I felt a weird sort of twist in my stomach, a tiny nervous twinge.

Slowly untangling her fingers from her hair, Rattles sniffed and dragged her sleeve across her snotty nose.

Shar pressed her cigarette into the plate she'd perched on the windowsill, snapping it in two.

Finally, because I had no idea what else to do, I popped up from my place on the floor, declaring, "I'm going to get you a tissue."

Outside, I took another long look down the hall, listened for the sound of other people, the sound of someone, anyone, with a vested interest in helping the crying girl in Shar's room.

Nothing.

I walked as slowly as I could to the bathroom, weighing each step, thinking, or hoping, that by the time I got back Rattles would have obediently disappeared.

I was standing with one hand on Shar's doorknob, a wadded-up handful of toilet paper in the other, when

I heard a splintering noise, like the sound of a foot going through a brittle floorboard.

When I pushed open the door, Shar was sitting on her bed, hairbrush in one hand, sleeve pulled back to display a red welt on her forearm.

"See?" she said, rubbing her fingernail over her raised skin. "No big deal."

Rattles seemed transfixed.

"Right, Allison?"

Before I knew it, Shar was up and had my arm in her grip, the brush raised. I could feel Rattles watching us, hear her raspy, post-crying breathing.

"Right, Allison?"

Truth or dare.

Which, like I said, I'd never played. Until Shar.

"Right?"

Her eyes still focused on me, Shar tightened her fingers around my wrist. She was pulling, a little, and smiling this familiar smile, like the smirk girls give each other when they've just said something mean about someone else, like the sly, no-tooth grin girls use when they're playing a game, a trick. It's the look of an accomplice. The look you give to your accomplice. Me.

"Right," I breathed.

Right answer.

SMACK!

I jolted. Shar held her grip firm for a moment as the sting spread across the flesh of my forearm.

I pulled my arm away and looked down to see Rattles hiking her grubby sweatshirt sleeves up.

Seeing Rattles's arms bared, Shar let out a sharp laugh, tossed the hairbrush on the bed.

"Or, yeah, you know? Or you could just study and take the exam I guess," she chuckled.

Rattles had gone stone quiet. She opened her hand, flicked the pills still stuck there onto the floor. "I should go," she said.

No one moved.

"Okay then," Shar chirped. "Good luck with your studies!"

"How many times," Rattles whispered thoughtfully, "do you think ... Like, to actually miss an exam. How many times would you, like, do it?"

"Theoretically," Shar added.

"Yeah."

"Maybe twenty-five?" Shar's voice was smooth and level. "What do you think, Allison? Theoretically?"

"I don't know," I stuttered. "Like ten?"

"Ten?" Shar coughed incredulously.

"Fifty?"

Shar raised an eyebrow, lit another smoke, and took a long inhale. After a few drags she rested her cig on the plate and walked toward Rattles, who was clearly lacking in momentum. "Come on, I'll walk you to your room."

They were gone for a while, especially considering that Rattles lived next door. It was long enough for me to open my textbook and take up a purely aesthetic pose, "studying" what from a glance seemed an impossibly long list of all the languages spoken by "Chinese" people.

At one point I thought I heard Shar tell Rattles to stop crying. It was hard to hear, though. And I kind of didn't want to listen.

Shar slid back into the room just as I was tracing my finger over a line about the Mongols, which I had clearly at some point thought was interesting enough to highlight with neon pink. She walked up behind me and stabbed the tip of her toe into the small of my back.

"Fifty! What are you, some kind of monster? Man! She's going to break her arm!"

"What do you mean?"

"You're terrible, Allison." She said it like she was describing a rock star, or something sweet and fattening. You're TERRIBLE, Allison.

"She's not going to DO it."

"Oh no?"

Shar got down next to me, knee on my textbook, and took my arm in her hands. "Look at your poor little bruise," she mocked. "Maybe you'll have to miss YOUR exam, bully."

"It's not even a bruise."

"You want me to kiss it better?"

That same smile.

"No!" I said, maybe a little too fast and too loud.

"As if," she cooed, planting a loud smooch on the pink outline the brush had left behind.

The next day I slept in and had to make a mad dash

to the auditorium for my East Asian History exam. The last question involved drawing a map of China. AN ENTIRE MAP. I drew a half-hearted rectangle with jagged edges and added in some rivers where I could remember there being rivers. Later on I found out that someone had taped a map to the back of the third toilet in the women's bathroom. So apparently there are a few reasons to stay in touch with your classmates.

I saw Rattles in the hallway before I heard the news. She was walking stooped, bent almost to a ninety-degree angle. Paler than ever with black circles under her eyes. She had a tensor bandage wrapped around her right wrist, a flesh-coloured wrap wound so thick it looked like a turnip.

"What happened to Ra— Nat?" I asked Carly, who was sitting on the floor in her room, surrounded by a sea of Cultural Studies notes I was hoping to borrow.

"She hurt her wrist." Carly shrugged, not looking up, twirling a highlighter in her fingers.

"Doing what?" I tried to perch myself on Carly's bed without disturbing what seemed to be a delicate study system.

Carly's walls were covered in black and white movie posters—all of them movies you'd have to rent at some obscure retro place to watch. I wondered if she had. Rented them.

She shrugged. "I don't know actually. I mean, I guess it was from practising too much because she plays piano, right? Hmmmm. Did you download the videos for Cultural Studies, because you need those too."

I got the whole story from Shar during her celebratory feast at Chicken! Chicken!

"Well she's TELLING PEOPLE that she tripped and fell. That girl is such a liar."

"What happened?"

"What do you think? She beat her fucking wrist! With a stapler!" Shar chuckled. "A STAPLER! Can you imagine? Guess someone didn't have a BRUSH!"

"WHAT?"

Pausing over her plate, Shar tapped her fork on her wrist in demonstration. "You know, like BANG BANG BANG!"

"She actually did it."

"Of course. Because she's a spineless pushover and I—WE—gave her a genius way to get out of her exam. Although"—Shar picked up a bit of chicken finger and proceeded to drown it in ketchup—"I'll say this, Rattles outdid herself. She CHIPPED a bone."

"NO!"

"Yep."

Watching Shar suck the ketchup off her chicken finger, it occurred to me that she was kind of glowing, with a look on her face like a mom holding up her kid's first-place ribbon. In front of her a feast of french fries lay smothered under a bloody blanket of ketchup. One of the fries was poking through like a bone splinter. Sort of.

The sickly sweet smell of tomato and the image of that little fry was making my stomach hurt.

"Wow. So. Huh."

It was hard not to picture Rattles alone in her room, maybe sitting on the bed next to her stapler. Her face all sweaty from constant crying. No one around to buy her chips and tell her to chill out, that exams are no big deal.

"I feel bad," I said, twirling the straw of my Coke.

"Why?"

"Because ..."

"Allison. We did not do anything to that girl, okay? Not that she didn't WANT us to, the lazy slug. Like we're going to do her dirty work for her. Like we're going to leave the door open for her to charge us with ASSAULT."

"She WANTED you—she wanted US—to hit her?"

Shar shrugged. "Who knows WHAT that girl wanted? Look, whatever you do, do not feel bad for the Rattles of this world. Maybe this will teach her not to wander around the halls sobbing and looking for sympathy."

On the way home, Shar demonstrated Rattles's wrist-banging technique on various surfaces. The railing on the steps outside the restaurant. A tree down the street from residence.

"Like this so BANG BANG BANG BANG!"

"Problem," I finally said.

"HA!" Shar hollered. "Are you kidding? Oh poor little Rattles can't handle exams! Oh poor Rattles! Let's all FEEL SO SORRY for her. Poor Rattles and her DEADLY office supplies! Fuck. It might just be the funniest thing I've heard this year. Oh! Do you think she did it fifty times? Is fifty enough to chip bone?"

"I don't know."

"Allison"—grabbing me by both shoulders, Shar pressed her forehead against mine—"you must RELAX and enjoy this moment with me!"

I could almost taste the red candy she was sucking on. Cherry.

The rest of my exams, after that, were a bit of a blur.

Linguistics was multiple choice; that is, the choice between a bunch of things I didn't recognize (so not much of a choice, really). Thankfully the Cultural Studies exam had an option to write about the one movie I'd managed to attend. Social Problems was an essay on a specific social problem; I chose sex. Shar finished her essay in fifteen minutes. I ended up sitting next to Jonathon, who was still there when I left. It looked like he was writing a novel.

The night before students left for Christmas break, each floor in the whole dorm had a secret holiday elf gift exchange. A stack of presents sat by the elevator in a cardboard box, cryptically labelled.

I'd gotten Carly, so I bought her a little magnet that looked like a Super 8 camera. Someone got me a giant chocolate A. Shar got a massive bottle of bubble bath.

"Because I take soooooo many baths," she drawled.

Shar was supposed to get a gift for Rattles, but when she walked down the hall she noticed a huge pile of presents with Rattles's name on them in the box.

"Fuck that," Shar said.

So we snuck into the St. Joseph's Debate Society Karaoke, which had made the mistake of stuffing a flyer into Shar's mailbox, and drank what would have been Rattles's present instead.

Shar said the last thing Rattles needed was more sympathy, let alone a bottle of Amaretto.

The karaoke night was a RETRO SPECIAL. We stayed for three versions of Journey's "Don't Stop Believin'," an extremely shrill rendition of Bob Marley's "No Woman No Cry," Black Sabbath's "Iron Man," one too many interpretations of Rush's "Tom Sawyer," and four rounds of Heart's "Barracuda."

"JeSUS we just HEARD this song," Shar would scream after every encore. "YOU GUYS SUCK!"

Every three songs we went up to the MC and requested the Rolling Stones until the DJ refused to talk to us anymore.

When we got back to residence, someone had gift-wrapped Rattles's door in pink paper and bows. Shar tore a ribbon off and stuck it on my head.

"Merry Christmas, Sonny."

Later, sitting on her bed watching *Jaws*, Shar held my arm in her lap and drew fifty tiny x's around my wrist.

Shar's train home left at nine the next morning. I walked her to the station through the first few flakes of snow as they drifted down like tiny paper airplanes. The station was a cloud of white noise and bustling bodies, like Grand Central, like you see in the movies.

As soon as we got in line to pick up her ticket, Shar changed. I kept waiting for her to say something shitty about all the slacker students in their track pants waiting in line. Shar hated track pants. But she just stood there, holding her coffee, looking off in the distance.

"You should go back and pack," she said when we first got in line, although it seemed more of a descriptive phrase than a request.

"No, it's okay. I'll wait. I mean, unless you want to be by yourself?"

"Why would I want to be by myself?"

When they called her train I reached over and kind of side-grabbed her in an awkward hug. It was like hugging a tree, hard and stiff. The crowd inched forward and Shar gave me a little push.

"Okay. Bye."

"See you soon," I offered. "Two weeks!"

"Uh-huh."

I watched her figure get smaller and smaller as she followed the line toward the train, catching sight of what looked like a tiny wave before she disappeared.

On the way home on my own train, later that night, I heard this girl telling her friend about a student who

got out of her American Civil War exam by going to
the dean and saying that exams were making her feel
depressed and overly anxious.

"So they let her off," the girl said, waving her
hands in the air, "just like that! They took her to
a counsellor and she got a note and wrote a paper
instead. Amazing, huh?"

Wrapping the scarf Shar had left in my room around
my face, I closed my eyes and tried to push myself
into sleep. Shar's x's faded into a soft purple that
circled my wrist like an old injury.

NINE

Break and split

Going home felt like a humongous waste of time.
I had basically no desire to see my parents (that
sounds harsh but it's true). It wasn't as if I'd spent
any time at St. Joseph's missing my home or my
neighbourhood or high school. If anything, I'd just
started feeling like I'd managed to escape that stuff.

Like, you know, thank GOD.

Of course, the first thing my mom noticed at the train
station was the scratch Shar had left on my burn
Halloween night.

By dinner she was picking and poking at me, pulling
on my shirt to expose the borders of old wounds.

She was all over me to go to the doctor. Like,
immediately. Like let's all overreact and call an
ambulance why don't we?

"It doesn't really look like you're looking after it."

"Mom! It's nothing! I had this HUGE scab and now I have this teeny tiny sore bit—"

"It *is* sore then," my dad noted.

For fuck's sake.

"Dad. It's a BURN. It doesn't TICKLE."

Overall, my parents noticed that I looked way paler than I did when I left. My dad said I had dark circles under my eyes, which he guessed was from partying.

"You know, there was this kid in my school who got scurvy when he was a freshman because he only ate beer and mac 'n' cheese," he noted.

"I don't have scurvy, Dad."

Halfway through dinner Shar called and I ran up to my room to take it.

Shar's mom lived on the west coast and her dad lived in England.

"The fact that I'm spending my Christmas NOT in England with my dad should tell you something about my parents' shitty power struggle," she'd explained a week before going.

On the phone she sounded tinny and thin.

"Well, Allison, I actually don't even have anything to say to you. Weird. Are you having fun?"

"Fun?"

"Clearly it's a stupid question, Allison. My mom is downstairs and I don't feel like dealing with her. So, make some small talk with me so I have something to do before I go out."

"You're going out?"

"Well I'm not staying here, am I?"

"Um. Okay. My parents think I'm not looking after myself. Whatever. I don't even feel like talking to them."

I don't know why I was being so pissy about my parents. Kind of a stereotype when you think about it.

"Where's your sister?" I asked.

"What?"

"Your sister. Is she at your mom's too?"

There was a pause and a thump on the other end of the phone. The sound of a door clicking closed.

"No. She's with my dad."

"In England."

"Right. Whatever. Let's stop talking about our stupid families, shall we? What else are you doing over there?"

"Nothing mostly, I guess." I tried to visualize myself doing things in the one day I'd been home. All I could see was myself sitting on the couch. Boring. "Watching TV. Eating my parents' food. You know."

"Right. Okay. Well. That's pretty fucking boring, Allison."

I searched my brain for something interesting to say that would keep Shar on the line.

"I'm supposed to make a Christmas list."

"Oh yeah? What are you going to ask for?"

"I dunno. Books I guess. Maybe a gift certificate?"

"Jesus, Allison. What are you, some high school nerd? Forget it." Shar suddenly sounded remotely chipper. "I'll email you your list tonight."

"What am I getting?"

"Well I don't know, Sonny, I guess you're just going to have to wait and see."

The list arrived the next day, attached to an empty email. I handed it over to my mom without even really looking at it.

Most of the stuff ended up being things that looked to me like Shar things. Fancy skinny-leg jeans, a black sweater with a big open neck, a scarf that reminded me of one of Shar's I still had stored in my pocket. There was perfume and some fancy kit for trimming your eyebrows and a book about this artist guy who staged car crashes.

My mom was kind of happy about it Christmas morning, watching me open all these cool gifts that to her suggested, I don't know, the possibility that I wouldn't be dressing like a slob anymore. "Well you look lovely!" she cooed. "I didn't even know you liked these kinds of jeans. Does this mean I can throw out those ugly old sweatshirts too?"

"NO."

The pants were a little tight, but they at least made me look like I had some sort of shape. I looked older. Standing in front of my mom's full-length mirror, I pictured me standing next to Shar, watching people go by. The two of us in our black outfits, me watching people from under my newly groomed eyebrows.

Two days later, when my mom asked about going on a shopping trip to buy more nice clothes, I let it slip about Shar and the list. This, for some reason, totally pissed my mom off. It turned on pissed-off like a switch or something. She was cooking and she kind of slammed the spoon she was using down on the counter.

"What do you mean, 'Shar wrote the list'?"

"What I said. Like, WROTE it."

"Shar. This is your new friend, Shar. Shar wrote your Christmas present list."

"YES. So what?"

"So what? Allison! So what that someone else wrote out the list of things you'd be getting for Christmas?"

"Yeah. So?"

"Allison." Towelling off her hands, my mom took a long look at me. "It's strange. Aren't you your own person?"

"What? Of COURSE I am! FUCK!"

"Don't say 'FUCK' to me, young lady."

"Okay. Geez. I'm so sorry I let a friend pick out MY presents."

My mom sighed.

I stormed off.

Although I guess I wasn't planning on talking to Shar a lot while I was home, it was weird that I heard from her as little as I did. After the first phone call, she mostly only texted and not every day. She sounded busy, like she was being absorbed into another really amazing life, which was probably more interesting, I thought, than hanging out with me in her dorm room all day.

I thought of calling when I found out my marks. Mostly because it seemed like kind of amazing news; by some miracle, I'd passed everything but East Asian History, which was a year-long course. I did well in Social Problems (B–) and okay in Cultural Studies (C–), which was, I'm sure, mostly because of Carly's notes. I got a D– in Linguistics, which was not so surprising.

When I texted Shar to tell her I passed (Cheers for Not Failing First Semester!!!!) I got this:

Wow aren't you special

The same day, Carly emailed to see how I'd done in Cultural Studies, attaching a photo of her skiing with her family at Whistler. Her entire family was the same size and shape. It was kind of hilarious.

I sent her a message saying that I'd passed and that her family looked like a set of Barbie dolls. She sent me back another picture of them looking even more blond, all standing in a row in front of a chalet in matching blue and yellow ski scarves and mittens.

We're the Swedish Ski team!!!! Too Funny! ☺

The day before I went back to school my parents finally dragged me to Dr. Zygiel, who kind of poked at the skin on my neck for a half hour.

"Well," he said, tapping on my burn with a gloved finger, "it looks like someone needs to be a little more careful."

Shar's scratch was infected, requiring a new round of antibiotic cream.

"Here's the rule, kiddo: if it hurts, don't ignore it. Pain is a message."

"Right."

"Can I get you anything else while you're here? How is your anxiety these days? Still having attacks?"

"Uh. No."

The only other thing I can say about Christmas break, which as you can tell was oh so interesting and illuminating, is that the second-to-weirdest part involved the conversation I had on the train ride back to school with the top hat guy, Jonathon. Who wasn't wearing his top hat, incidentally.

Which is maybe why, at first, I didn't realize who he was. I just noticed a guy reading this book from our Social Problems class, *Discipline and Punish*. It's not a dirty book, in case you were wondering. From what I'd managed to read first term, it was kind of interesting but kind of hard to understand.

Five minutes after the train left the station, Jonathon dropped his book and burst into a big smile. "Well, greetings! Allison, correct?"

"Oh. Yeah."

"Seems a bit serendipitous we keep running into each other like this."

"I guess."

Or we just live in the same city, I grumbled mentally.

"Well," Jonathon chuckled, cracking the spine of his book a little, "if you akin yourself to those sorts of notions of the order of the universe. Either that or we live in the same town and just happen to go to the same school."

"Sure."

It was funny to see someone so seemingly overjoyed to bump into you. It made me wonder just how unpopular Jonathon was.

I mean, top hat, bad skin, talks like a weirdo, reads books even after the class is done.

Odds were, not that popular.

When he noticed me eyeing his book, he held open a page and pointed at a Post-it. "My JIs."

"What?"

"JI. Jonathon's Insights. My moments of revelation, as it were. Points of interest for the scholar and generally curious folk."

"Oh."

He talked my ear off for almost an hour, mostly about Social Problems, which, apparently, he LOVED. "A fascinating lecture series, I thought. Not your typical 101 drivel with its survey and overarching considerations of the human experience. Some real 'aha' moments from the great Professor Jawari. The old gal has a wicked sense of humour. Did you know she studied serial killers in Canada for a spell?"

A *spell*?

"Fascinating."

Looking at Jonathon's skin up close, it was hard not to stare. Like, you think I'm exaggerating when I say how bad it was. I'm not. His face looked like the bottom of a deep fryer. Plus he had this crazy unibrow that looked like a face hedge. As a side note, sitting this close to him I noticed that his breath smelled like hot cinnamon gum with an undertone of sour cream and onion.

My dazed stare was interrupted by the sudden thought that it was entirely possible people who talked to ME were looking at the gross skin on MY neck and thinking something like the same fricking thing.

Across the aisle I could see a couple watching us. It occurred to me, I guess, that from a close distance we were this weird-looking couple, with collectively horrible skin.

"Uh, Jonathon. I think I'm going to put my headphones on. If that's cool."

"Oh of course! I will make sure as not to disturb your slumber. I'm just going to be here reading. Don't you mind me."

"Great."

For the rest of the ride, every time I looked up to check on Jonathon he was looking down at me. Eventually I just squeezed my eyes shut and pretended I was in some sort of non-anaesthetized surgery.

At the station, Jonathon followed me out of the train and then asked if we could share a cab. I lied and said I was walking.

"Okay, well. I'll see you in class I presume? That is, depending on what you have planned for yourself for this semester." Jonathon's bag was one of those old-man suitcases: all brown vinyl with a big buckle holding everything together. He'd tied a string to it and kept twisting it around his wrist. Twisting and untwisting. Nervously.

"Uh. Yep. Okay. Bye."

"Adieu."

I don't know why I felt I couldn't get away from him fast enough, but I couldn't. I practically bolted to the street to catch a cab, the wheels of my suitcase clicking furiously.

When I got back to dorm Shar was waiting, leaned up against my door with her headphones on; I caught sight of her shape before I saw her face. Then of course I saw her face and totally spazzed out.

"WHAT HAPPENED?"

Shar smiled, a flat, lips-together smile, and the massive split that dissected her bottom lip in two gaped purple. Like a blueberry. A blueberry on a vanilla sundae.

"Dump your bags, Allison. We're going out."

We ended up at Funxion, an aging punk rockers' bar covered in rusted spikes and peeling red paint. Inside it was lukewarm: lukewarm music murmuring through a set of fuzzy speakers hanging from the ceiling, lukewarm beer smell wafting through the air. The tables were all covered in red plastic tarps that stuck to my arms like fly tape. Mostly the place was full of really old-looking punks, sitting alone in their black T-shirts with their beers. We took a seat by the window. Shar cupped her hands around the glass candle on the table and pulled the light under her chin, illuminating the cut on her lip and making her skin glow yellow.

The bartender squinted at my ID, then tossed it back on the table.

"What can I get you … Jennifer?"

"Two—"

"Rum and Cokes," Shar interrupted.

When someone doesn't want to talk to you they look up or they look down, at the floor, at the ceiling, at the placemat, at the sky. Sometimes they look at a non-existent person standing behind and to the left of you. Shar looked at the flickering light of the candle cupped in her hands. At the sputtering speakers.

I looked at Shar. I couldn't think of anything to say. Finally, I told her about Jonathon and the ride up on the train.

Shar nodded. "Oh yeah. I know Jonathon."

"You know Jonathon?" Disbelief burped out of me like the casing of a sunflower seed.

"Allison. Hello? We're in the same class."

"Right. Just. You talked to him?"

"Of course. Once or twice. His face is totally disgusting."

I tried to picture a moment where I'd seen Shar talking to anyone.

"Whatever, Allison," she sneered. "It's not like we're attached at the hip and you're with me every minute. I think I talked to him once at the beginning of term."

Shar used a straw to sip her rum and Coke, served in a sticky beer stein, careful to avoid the centre of her lip.

I got this sudden vibe like I was the last person she wanted to talk to.

This was not how I'd pictured my first hangout with Shar after Christmas. Although, I guess the obvious question would be, What *did* I expect Shar to be like? That she'd be all bubbly? Or notice that I was wearing the outfit she'd pretty much ordered for me for Christmas?

In the interest of both changing what was feeling

like a weird subject and addressing a subject I was genuinely curious about, I pointed at my lip and raised my eyebrows.

Shar continued to sip.

"So. So what happened?" I asked.

"What always happens," she shrugged, "when I get together with my stupid ex who I should learn to just avoid because he's a plague."

"He HIT you?"

Shar paused and sipped. Then, finally, she looked up at the ceiling, sighed, and said, "I'm not nice to him, Allison. Whatever. We're not nice to each other. We've been through too much shit and now just, like, being in the same room with him is bad news."

"Problem," I joked low.

Shar took a loud straw-slurping sip of her drink, digging through the ice a bit. "A pretty fucking serious problem, Allison."

"I'm sorry. I don't know anyone who's ever been hit by a guy before I guess."

"Welcome to adulthood. This stuff happens, Allison. It happens to everyone."

Outside the window, oatmeal-sized snowflakes were starting to fall. An old man sitting three tables over started singing along with the music on the jukebox, which I only then just noticed.

"Mirror in the bathroom ..."

Shar shook up the ice in her drink and stared out the window.

"You want another drink?" I asked.

"Clearly."

I bought two more drinks, then two more.

A little after midnight, Shar leaned forward and put her chin on the table, reaching her tongue out to carefully poke at the sore spot on her lip, not unlike the way a kid pokes at the hole where a tooth has fallen out.

She chuckled. Her eyes flashed up toward the ceiling. "Rick Rick Rick Rick Rick ..."

"Who is Rick?"

"Nooooo oooonnnnne."

"Is he the guy who hit you—is Rick?" My head swirled with successive drinks.

Sitting up, Shar waved her hands frantically in front of her face, like someone being attacked by a herd of invisible bees. "ARG! Forget it! Forget I said his name. Okay, no more saying his fucking name."

"Right. Just. Okay. But is this, um, the guy who beat you up before?"

"Yeah." Snapping up in her seat, Shar slammed her hand on the table, jostling our drinks into spilling their guts. "What? Yes. Wait. I told you about him?"

"You said something. Last month."

"Okay. No more talking about R— THE GUY."

By two a.m., the crabby bouncer-type in a black leather vest and a belt made of bullets had poured us out onto the streets. Shar grabbed my arm.

"Oh, Sonny. What oh what are we going to do to keep ourselves amused THIS term?"

Overhead, the streetlights swarmed like low-lit comets.

Her hair smelled like lavender. Like the smell you'd smell if you were lying in a field of lavender on a sunny day. Or something. "Whatever you want," I said.

At the dorm, in the elevator on the way up, Shar pinned me to the wall, pushed a finger in my chest.

"YOU," she said, "NEVER called. All vacation. HA!"

"What?" I gasped. Her lips were dizzyingly close as she leaned in.

"Whatever." And just like that, she pushed away from me. Yawned. "Come get me tomorrow. I'm gonna need a greasy breakfast."

"Okay."

"I knew that sweater would look awesome. Night."

It occurred to me, as I collapsed on the bed next to my unpacked suitcase, that I had a class at eight-thirty a.m.

Or was it nine-thirty a.m.?

"Oh well," I muffled into my pillow and let sleep grab me from the back of my head like a wrestler.

SECOND TERM

HEALTH AND WELLNESS AT ST. JOSEPH'S!

Attention Dylan Hall Residents!

Consider this year a chance to make new, healthy choices part of your student life at St. Joseph's. Below are just a few of the ways you can make your freshman year a safe, healthy, and happy one!

1. **EAT HEALTHY! Learn proper portion size, avoid fatty foods and late-night snacking!**

2. **DRINK LESS! Remember, you don't have to drink to have a good time with your friends!**

3. **EXERCISE! St. Joseph's has many athletic programs available to students. Join a team! Take a class! Make a new friend!**

4. **SLEEP! Studies show students on average sleep less than five hours a night. Get to bed early and you'll feel better in the morning! Avoid all-nighters!**

Remember, mental and physical health is an important part of your success at St. Joseph's College.

Study hard. Have fun. Stay safe!

TEN

Things that change

Second term. Introduction to Women's Studies.
Departmental Survey of English Literature. Cultural
Studies (Part II). East Asian History (Part II). Critical
Thinking, a recommended follow-up to Social
Problems, which Shar refused to take because, she
said, "I AM a fucking critical thinker, Allison. What
are they going to teach me that I don't already know?"

And.

Go.

Partying geared back up immediately. Just about
every conversation I heard in the hallway the first
week back sounded something like this (please note
the lack of names or boy/girl references, as this
conversation was had by people of all types all over
college, from Pizza Hut to the third-floor laundry
room of Dylan Hall):

"Dude, are we GOING out tonight or fucking WHAT?"

"OH! Dude, we are GOING to drink tonight my fine friend. WE are getting wasted."

"WASE-TED!"

(High fives.)

"My tolerance is in the shitter dude."

"That can be mended my friend. Totally mended."

Aside from the familiar sights and sounds of dudes and chicks getting "wase-ted," there were some subtle but notable changes in the St. Joseph's student body second term. When I say "body," I am not actually referring to the infamous "freshman fifteen" and the fact that, okay, sure, people did seem to be a little bit chubbier by January. I didn't think it was that big a deal, although, clearly, other people did: shortly after classes resumed, the local athletic supply store sold out of butt-shaping running shoes and the cafeteria started selling diet pop almost exclusively. Campus was flooded with flyers for aerobic boot camps, toning classes, and Weight Watchers groups.

At Dylan, the Patties had *lost* a ton of weight (on what was likely a patty-only diet) since September. They'd also traded in their cartoon tees and sweats for black-only yoga gear. They looked like ninjas, like two thoroughbreds waiting for a starter pistol.

"Jesus Christ," Shar hissed, passing them in the hallway, "those bitches look like a couple of cats that just came out of the bathtub. Pretty soon it'll be feeding-tube time."

The Patties' new skinniness made Shar hate them even more. I personally wouldn't have thought this was possible, given that we'd never really spoken to either of them. Not that that mattered to Shar, who took up the practice of stalking the Patties, a task that involved long walks in the cold, four paces back.

It wasn't exactly subtle.

Finally, after a particularly long stalk through campus, Mini Patty spun around and gave us the finger. There were tears in her eyes. Just little tears that could have been her eyes watering, but I don't think so. It was kind of horrifying looking at her as she glared at us, shivering in the white cold. Shar laughed.

"Shar," I whispered, "let's go. Okay? Shar?"

"Fine."

That was the seed of one of our first fights. That night at dinner, after sitting for ten minutes in chilly silence over grilled cheese and fries, Shar snapped.

"Allison? When you say stuff like 'Shar let's go' it's a bit like saying 'Shar you're being an asshole,' okay, and I don't appreciate it."

"Sorry."

"Why are you sorry? You don't get anything. You don't know anything."

If everyone else at Dylan was focused on change in relation to fat (gained or lost), the change I worried about second semester was the one I saw in Shar, mostly in relation to her mood. Which is to say that second semester Shar seemed to be mad. Like, more than usual. If that was at all possible.

I mean, okay, Shar, as long as I'd known her, pretty much hated almost everyone. But for the most part, like, up until Christmas, I'd been under the impression that she also didn't really give a shit about anyone. So no one ever really got to her, you know?

But after Christmas break, Shar seemed to think that everyone was somehow fucking with her, like they were being mean to her. And everything bothered her. And everyone.

Even me.

Maybe especially me.

It seemed that Shar and I were always on the verge of a fight. It was like one of those bad smells you notice in a restaurant and try to ignore, but can't.

And then it all got, like, bad. On a day that had been kind of ordinary.

It was a Wednesday, I think. This was after Mini Patty gave us the finger. It was a day that had distinguished itself only because I'd finally managed to force myself to go to Critical Thinking class that started at ten-thirty a.m.

Who can think critically at ten-thirty a.m.?

Not me.

After finding a seat at the back of the lecture hall, I promptly fell asleep (because I'd been up till four the night before, watching *Six Feet Under* and eating packages of uncooked ramen noodles in Shar's room). In what felt like seconds and was actually an hour later, I bolted awake to find two copies of an assignment outline that had been shoved under my sleeping face. Class dismissed.

Shar was supposed to meet me on the steps of the main college building after class. So there I was, waiting, about to check my phone, when I heard these oddly familiar voices arguing over my shoulder.

"I wouldn't."

"Why not? What's she like, some sort of jerk? Is she a total bitch? She doesn't look like a bitch."

"OH, just ask her. SHE'S not going to bite your head off."

I turned around and it was the Patties, in matching yoga uniforms, standing with this other girl with a bright orange bushel of curly hair tucked under a fluffy white hat. She had the most amazing eye makeup I'd ever seen.

"YO," the girl said, stepping forward. "So sorry to bug you, but, um, I'm Jewel. And, uh, I was wondering if, uh. Do you happen to have a copy of the assignment for Critical Thinking? I think you're in my class? I flaked and didn't grab one of the sheets so ..."

"Uh, yeah." Rummaging in my bag, I pulled out a crumpled assignment and, quickly checking for drool marks, handed it over. "Take this one. I got two for some reason."

"AMAZING. Are you taking the class? I know a lot of people are dropping it because of the exam."

"Um. I don't know. It's super early. Or, I mean, like, it feels super early. I guess ten-thirty isn't early."

"JEWEL!" Mini Patty stood straddling several steps, hands on hips. "If we're going to Hot Yoga we gotta go now."

"'Kay. Well. THANKS!" Throwing a giant wave in my direction, the Patties and the girl with the pumpkin hair disappeared.

After that, I must have waited twenty minutes on the steps. Finally I called Shar to see where she was.

"What?"

"Hey, where are you?"

"Eating."

"I thought you were supposed to meet me."

"I'm at Sam's."

CLICK.

She was almost finished when I got there. I slid into the booth just as the waitress was leaving the bill.

"What happened?" I asked quietly.

"Nothing. You just looked like you were having lots of fun with the Patties, so ..."

"What? I didn't even see you! I was just giving this girl something for the class."

"So you say."

She stood up and stormed out of the restaurant. And of course I followed her.

"Shar! What is wrong?!"

She chugged forward, punching her way through the busy street. "Nothing, Allison. Except I'm starting to get this feeling like maybe I can't trust you."

"WHAT?" People stopped and stared. "SHAR! SHAR WAIT! WHY?"

She stopped so quickly I skidded into her—and then she shoved me, hard enough that I almost tipped off the sidewalk.

"HEY!"

"DON'T yell at me, Allison. I'm telling you that when I see you on the steps fucking yukking it up with the fucking veggie Patties and their fucked-up friends just like DAYS after you're all up in my face for no reason because you think I'm hurting their feelings, I'm a bit like what the fuck."

"Okay. Okay, I'm sorry."

"You're not. You're all like, 'Shar, it's no big deal.'"

"Okay."

"Stop saying 'okay.' Every time you say 'okay' it makes me think you're full of shit."

"Oka—" I clamped my hands over my mouth. The word "okay," for the record, is a very hard word to stop saying once you've started.

Shar's eyes narrowed. She turned and walked away. I followed her a few car lengths behind. About a block away from campus she shook me off, disappearing around a corner.

Instead of going back to campus I headed to the food court at the underground mall, which seemed like a suitable place to go at the time. It was the least popular mall in the city as far as most college students were concerned. Its stores sold only weird combinations of plastic, hardware, and housewares. The food court had almost no green food for sale.

I went to Wok? Wok? Wok! and ordered chicken balls, fried rice, and spare ribs, all in varying shades of the same overcooked brown. I was sitting on my orange plastic chair reassessing this order when a familiar voice dropped onto my shoulder.

"Hey, you!"

The person who seemed the most outwardly changed since first term was Carly. During Christmas break she'd gotten all her hair cut off into what looked like a faux hawk. She'd stopped wearing pink and yellow entirely and started wearing these really retro-looking stiff blue jeans and white T-shirts, kind of like what she wore to the Halloween party. I wonder if that's where she got the idea. She looked like some sort of fifties-dude pin-up, complete with a studded biker jacket.

"Allison! What's up?"

I pointed at my Styrofoam plate and shrugged.

Carly grinned. "Isn't this mall great? When the apocalypse happens we can all live underground and we'll never go hungry. Soooooo. Where's your BFF?"

"She's not here."

"You guys are like joined at the hip!" Carly chuckled, grabbing a seat and plunking her bags down around her.

"Contrary to popular opinion, there are some things we do apart."

Carly frowned. "I didn't mean to upset you."

"I'm not."

"Sorry." Carly bent over and began collecting the handles of her bags.

I could feel my face tightening, twisting into a position sufficient to hold back tears.

"No it's okay— It's fine. I'm sorry. I guess I'm in a bad mood."

Carly stood up. Put a hand on her hip and sighed. "Yeah. Okay. There's no way you're eating those toxic Oriental balls. I'm meeting Danny at the BEST french fry place, which is way better. Trust me. It will rock your world. Come eat with us. You'll love Danny."

Danny was easy to spot from a distance. He was like a cartoon character, six feet tall with a ducktail hairdo topping him off like a retro sundae. The upper half of his body was swamped in a fuzzy neon-blue sweater. As soon as he spotted us he started waving jubilantly. It was like he hadn't seen anyone in months, throwing his arms around Carly for a big hug and then turning to throw a grin in my direction.

"Hey, doll."

"Danny …" Disengaging from her welcome hug, Carly made a sweeping motion around my head. "This awesome lady is Allison."

"Oh YEAH. Hey, Allison. Didn't you come to the first film thing?"

"Yeah."

"I remember you. Yeah. You look like a character in a children's book I used to love. That's a compliment. Take it and put it in your pocket for later. Also. I love your hair. End of compliment session."

As soon as they'd ordered, Danny and Carly got down to business. The film club was in full steam, getting ready to start shooting scenes for their zombie musical, which Carly and Danny and Danny's partner Matt had written over Christmas break.

"Whatever happened to that other guy?" I finally cut in, once our fries had arrived. "The other, um, head film guy?"

"Oh, Dollywood. That dick. Had to go. A coup ensued. Victory was ours."

"Danny's kind of a film genius," Carly added, stabbing a fry with a plastic fork. "He's totally our leader now. He's our Wes Anderson."

"Oh? Cool."

"HONEY. I'm your Danny Maclane. That's who I am, baby. Wes Anderson can go blow himself."

Afterward Carly bought me an ice cream at a creepy Korean convenience store. It was already getting dark outside. It was also too cold for ice cream but Carly didn't seem to care.

"Hey so. If you're free. You should come to a film club meeting sometime. It's actually really cool."

"Yeah that sounds cool."

Peeling open her ice cream and licking the cotton-candy-blue top, Carly took a good long look at me. "Okay. Can I ask you something without sounding like an asshole? Like, with you understanding that I'm not being an asshole? I just want to know?"

"Sure. I guess. This is a really weird thing to be eating in the winter."

Carly stopped walking and sat on one of the little concrete college benches with positive learning affirmations engraved on top.

I never teach my pupils. I only attempt to provide the conditions in which they learn. —Albert Einstein

Sitting on "learn," I watched Carly's face as she formulated her question, her butt rocking back and forth on "pupils" as she shivered in the cold.

"Why do you think? Okay. Wait. Okay. Here it is. Why do you think that Shar, who I'm sure when she's with you is totally cool ... but ... why do you think she's so mean?"

"Because of what she said to um ... the yoga girls?"

Carly paused. "Yeah. Wow. Yeah. Sure. That and the other stuff."

Rattles. I couldn't remember her actual name so I didn't say anything. Maybe it wasn't Rattles.

"I don't know. People piss her off sometimes?"

"Allison, everyone gets pissed off. Shar's a perma-bitch. Like, someone says ONE thing to her and then for the rest of the year she's all up in their face? What's up with that?"

I pictured Shar sitting on her bed, curled up the way she usually was when we were hanging out. Carly made her sound like some sort of fairy-tale evil witch, which of course she totally wasn't.

"I guess some people, like, trigger stuff for her?" It occurred to me that Shar could be hiding in the shadows. I took a brief scan. "Her sister has an eating disorder," I whispered. "So. I think it makes her mad when people are all freaked out about food."

"Oh." Carly rubbed her hands together, popped the last bit of her blue ice treat in her mouth. "Okay. Well. Yeah, okay I guess. It's like, still, you know? It's still weird. But I didn't know about the eating disorder sister thing."

"Yeah well." I stood up. "Thanks for hanging out … and all that stuff."

"You okay?"

"Of course. See you later I guess."

"Bye!"

Street lamplights swung my shadow along the sidewalk, stretching the silhouette version of me to a breaking point and then snapping it back. A block away I could hear shrieks and giggles, the scraping of heels against pavement, the low rumble of idling cabs.

It was Wednesday, HUMP DAY, official slut night at Dylan Hall.

Something that was definitely not part of the "let's be healthy in second semester" St. Joseph's campaign.

Basically, even though technically every day of the week held the possibility of going out and getting shit-faced, no matter what, *everyone* went out on Wednesday: engineering students headed for the local beer and pizza place, the yoga heads chugged energy drinks and went clubbing, jocks headed for sports bars, and even the social work students went out (mostly to movies). That night the main hall was an overwhelming Pixies mix of loud and soft as girls called up to people to come downstairs ("Bitch, if you do not get down here this instant we are fucking OUT OF HERE"), fought about restaurants ("Oh my GOD PLEASE no more PIZZA") and bars ("Can we go someplace I can have WINE? Like, not just BEER?"), and fixed each other's hair. Two girls adjusted their gloss using the reflection in their phones. Hope, bundled in a massive orange down coat, brushed past me on my way to the elevator.

"Hey. Uh."

"Allison."

"Right. Allison. Have a good night, eh?"

On the landing of the sixth floor a bunch of Shar's floormates were all painted up and ready to go, anxiously bouncing around and talking about some guy some girl was going to fuck that night.

"Oh SUUUURE you're going to get laid. Right. My ASS."

"Shut up, Ashley!"

"I'm just going to get wasted and make out with some random guy."

"AGAIN! HAR HAR!"

Shar's door was closed.

"Shar?" I tapped. "Shar?"

I could hear what sounded like a fan going on the other side of the door. I was pressed up listening hard when Shar appeared behind me.

"What?"

It had occurred to me in the elevator on my way up that I'd never really fought with Shar, mostly because I'd never said or done anything to contradict her.

Standing in the frame of the bathroom door, Shar frowned. Her split lip was scabbed over now, a brown lump against pink. In her giant Madonna T-shirt, she shifted her hip to one side. Waiting.

"Um. I was just coming to see what you wanted to do tonight," I said.

"I don't feel like doing anything."

"Oh. Okay well. I guess I was just. I mean, do you want to get a movie? We could. Um. I mean I could even go and grab food if. I don't know if you ate. Um."

Here's something. You can talk and talk and talk and not get rid of silence.

"Or we could just sit and, I don't know if you want to study."

Sometimes silence sits on talk like a bully, squashing any power words might possibly have.

"Or we could go out? Or. You didn't want to do anything so …"

Shar's silence pushed on me the way a mattress pushes on you when you sleep. At some point she broke past me and into her room where she immediately flipped on her music and slammed the door shut.

I went upstairs to my room. More silence. I tried to think of things I needed to be doing. There were lots of things I could, and needed, to do without Shar, things I needed to be doing that I hadn't been doing for the past several months because somehow everything got sucked up by Shar.

I could do some work for some of my classes, for example. My Critical Thinking and Women's Studies course readers sat on my desk, still encased in their original cellophane.

I could call Carly, who had even kind of implied that she wanted to hang out with me. It seemed amazing to me that Carly had changed so much. I thought maybe it was the film guy, Danny, who seemed kind of cool. Maybe he'd, like, gone out and bought her a bunch of new clothes. Gay guys are always giving girls makeovers.

It's hard to do anything else when what you're really doing is waiting for a phone call, especially when you can't admit that's what you're doing. I didn't even realize I was holding my phone in my hand until I went to go turn on my computer to check my email.

No emails.

More silence.

I put my earphones on and curled up in bed. Music collected in my brain, pooled there.

I'm not sure when I fell asleep.

I dreamed I was in my old high school science class. Anne was there. I wanted to talk to her but I was afraid to. Then I remembered she wasn't talking to me anymore. That's when I noticed that I was on fire, blue flames snaking out of my fingers like ghosts, oozing out of my skin and bending like orange ferns around my arms. I tried to put my hands in my mouth to put out the flames. They tasted like smoke.

That's when I woke up, batted off my earphones, heard screaming outside.

"FIRE!"

ELEVEN

It's you. Again.

By law, every dorm floor at St. Joseph's must be
equipped with a fire extinguisher. At Dylan they were
in those glass cases on the wall by the elevator, next
to the sign that insisted you *not* take the elevator in
the case of a fire. Not even if you're really tired.

Since spotting ours the first day, I'd often stopped
to take a good long look. I thought of it less as pre-
emptive and more as just a practical thing for a girl
with my experience to know about. So. I knew how
the latch opened. (The door was secured with a little
plastic tag that was easy to rip.) Sometimes buildings
house these things behind glass you're supposed to
break to get in, which I suppose is to make sure that
it's really a serious fire and not something you could
snuff out with two wet fingers.

I've never had the opportunity to use a fire
extinguisher myself. I am, apparently, the person

who makes this kind of object necessary, but not the person who makes it useful.

Hope ended up using the fire extinguisher. She got off the elevator and immediately noticed the smell of smoke. She was about to bolt back down the stairs (bypassing the unrecommended elevator ride) when she noticed the fire extinguisher and decided it was worth at least checking to see if she could put out whatever was on fire.

The source of smoke and flame was Katy's door, which was covered not only in sticky notes but also photos—of Katy, her boyfriend, her new nephew, and a bunch of other people—and a giant whiteboard for people to leave "positive messages" on. Katy was sort of the unofficial person to talk to about problems in our dorm. She had the number of the Head of Residence as one of her Fav Five. People were always tacking their problems to her door. Someone had also left a garbage bag at the foot of her door earlier that night; in it were a sweater and some pants that had been damaged in the often-psychotic twists of the eighth-floor washing machine. It nearly killed Katy when someone, somehow, set it on fire and the bag leaked plumes of smoke into her room and mine. Katy slept soundly with the help of her ambient noise machine, so she didn't hear a thing until it was almost too late.

It was Hope I heard shouting "FIRE," whose shouting was eventually joined by Katy's screams and finally the screams of what sounded like two other girls. I remember smoke rushing into my lungs. I remember standing and suddenly feeling sick, sick like a dead pig must feel in the hot dark confines of a barbecue pit. I remember watching my hand grab the doorknob and being afraid it wouldn't turn. When I flung the door open, smoke still hovered in the air. The hallway was covered in white. Katy's knees cut long tracks through the mess of white foam as she crawled toward the stairwell in her long cotton nightgown, looking like Ophelia in her final days, mad hair and eyes, grey limbs. Hope dropped the extinguisher and hunched over her. Little bits of foam were stuck to Katy's hair. She was whimpering.

"Katy! Katy, stop! It's okay!"

The smoke ended up mostly affecting Katy's room and mine. Katy was taken to the hospital for smoke inhalation; the paramedics checked my vitals and then told me to take it easy and to come to the hospital if I had any symptoms, anything that seemed abnormal. One of them pointed at my scar and raised an eyebrow.

"Is THAT from a fire?"

"Not a big one," I replied.

Carly arrived a couple minutes after the fire department had gone downstairs to check on why the fire alarm hadn't gone off. She had to push her way through security.

"Um. WHAT THE FUCK?"

"Fucking FIRE!" Hope hollered over the shoulder of a security guard.

Seconds later, Carly stood next to me, peering into my room. It smelled like a bonfire.

"The alarm didn't go off," she said.

"No."

"Shit. Are you okay? Holy shit. A fire!"

Not a fire, I wanted to say. *Smoke.*

Girls trickled in from Hump Night adventures. Freaked out. Checked their rooms to make sure everything was still there and nothing had combusted or been stolen by flames.

A person in charge of college residence stuff appeared about an hour later with a book of cab chits and forms for us to sign relating to damage assessment. Residents on the eleventh floor were told to gather what they'd need to relocate for the night while the police and fire departments did an investigation.

"Of course, the college will provide housing for the evening."

"A hotel?" Hope asked hopefully.

"No."

I didn't want to go. I wanted to sit in the hallway and wait. Underneath my fingertips the hallway carpet fibres were sticky. Damp. Not good to sit on.

"Allison? Allison, where are you staying tonight?" Carly's voice was careful.

"I'm fine," I said, although of course I didn't feel fine.

"Okay. Come on," Carly coaxed, grabbing my elbow. "It's late. Let me take you to my friend Jay's house. Okay? Just for the night. He's got a huge apartment and you can sleep on his couch."

One or two people reached out to give me what I supposed were meant to be consoling touches on the shoulder. My head hurt, a light buzz of a hurt that hovered over me like a tilted halo while Carly guided me out down the stairs, onto the street, and into a cab.

My coat, my hair, my skin smelled like ashtray. When I closed my eyes I saw the shadow of my doorknob lightly outlined in the dark of my room. Right before I opened my eyes I fell forward as I mentally grabbed for that thin silver shape.

I jerked myself upright. Saw Carly.

"Wow sweetie, you look like shit. Do you want water or something? Okay, just try to relax."

I managed a quick "hello" to Jay before bolting past him and into the bathroom, where I immediately barfed my guts out. After that I lay on the floor listening to Carly in the hallway.

"Fire. Something something something something. Yeah, AGAIN."

A couple of minutes later, a scratch at the door.

"Allison? Allison are you okay? Should we take you to the hospital? Allison? Can you just like kick the door with your foot or something to let us know you're not passed out or in a coma?"

"I'm okay."

"Allison?"

"I'm OH KAY."

The linoleum was cold and comforting. It was dirty, covered in a sea of grey lint balls and smelling slightly of mildew, but also cold and comforting.

An hour later I made it to the couch. Carly made me a mug of camomile tea. She tried to get me to change my clothes. I refused. I wanted to be still. I pushed myself into the corner of the scratchy couch that smelled like mothballs. Every thought in my brain felt like it was blocks away, huffing through the cold, heading my way but still too far to hear. I fell asleep to a rerun of some cop show about an angry cop.

My phone buzzed at three-thirty a.m. Shar.

Are you ok? Where are you?

I stared at the glowing text for a while. Imagining what a concerned Shar would sound like.

At someone's house. Ok.

Seconds later.

Come here?

On the TV there was a commercial playing about an old person who was applying for life insurance. It occurred to me that it was strange for Shar to ask me, rather than tell me, to do something.

Although then I figured, Well, of course, she'd heard what happened.

Please.

It took me about five minutes to find my boots and coat, and then a piece of paper to leave a note for Carly saying I'd decided to go back to the dorm. I found the door and slipped out onto the street. The cold air felt good on my face, even if it was kind of insanely freezing. I dug out my mittens and covered my ears with my hands. I must have looked like someone walking away from an invisible shouting person, charging off in silent fury.

There was no one in the hallway, no one on the stairs. I slipped through the dorm like a burglar, touched Shar's door softly with the pad of my index finger.

"Shar," I whispered, suddenly worried that I'd hallucinated the call.

"Who is it?"

"Allison."

The door opened. Shar's face was wet, her features smudged and puffy, her hair pushed up on one side. She'd changed into a little black silk nightie that was crinkled and ripped a bit. It stuck to the skin of her stomach. She looked worried, worried but something else, too.

"It's you," she mumbled, words like fine fish hooks in the skin of my heart. The memory of Anne and her tiny lips forming over those words projected against the inside of my mind's iris.

Fucked up.

"Yeah."

"Are you okay?" she asked, in a tone that implied I was lying earlier.

Which, of course, I was. Everyone lies in text messages.

"Yeah. I mean. No. I'm just a little. I just don't feel ... you know ... really good."

There was a bottle of vodka on the floor by the bed. I had what felt like an obligatory swig while Shar puttered around, changing the music, going on and on about how everyone was freaking out, how people had gone down to the TV room and talked for hours about what had happened. She seemed happy then sad, singsongy and then suddenly lost.

I didn't know exactly what I was waiting for her to say.

"Are you okay?" I finally asked.

She collapsed on the bed, fell against me with a sigh.

"The world is fucked up, Sonny," she said.

"I guess."

"Sonny?" She put her hand on my face, just above my scar. I leaned into it, suddenly and impossibly wanting whatever it is people get out of having their face held like that.

"Yes."

"I just need you. Okay? I need you to be my friend. I mean really be my friend. No one is ever my friend."

Her kiss tasted like rust.

TWELVE

Rumour and insight

You know you have a problem because society tells you that you have a problem (see Social Problems lecture notes).

Society, in my experience, equals an army of mean people (mostly girls aged five to twenty-one) who get off talking about your problems. First, behind your back. Eventually, to your face.

My problems, my past, have been the source of a lot of talk over the few years of my existence. Like, how everyone in grade ten talked about the fact that I was the only virgin in 10B homeroom (not that that's a big PROBLEM if you think about it—it's grade TEN).

The worst rumour about me I ever heard was also the most stupid.

About a month after she disowned me as a friend, word circulated that I'd taken advantage of Anne. *Taken advantage of.* Like, how unchivalrous. Like I stole her credit card or had a party at her house and drank all her booze.

I found out about the rumour from this girl in our spare, Leslie Vanderhausen, when she kicked me out of our study group. Because of Anne.

"Look," she huffed, "FRANKLY, I don't want to get involved in any of this but I WILL say that *taking advantage* of someone like Anne, who was really nice to you, is crappy."

"Who said I *took advantage* of Anne?"

Of course, no one ever remembers who starts rumours, which makes them very much either like or unlike wars (depending on what history class you're taking).

I did eventually "talk" to Anne about this. I texted her with:

WHEN EXCTLY DID I TAKE ADVNTG OF U?

And she responded with:

DON'T KNOW WHAT UR TALKING ABOUT. STOP.

I remember looking at my phone that day and thinking that if I were a supporting character in a sitcom I'd kill myself over that text message.

Back at Dylan, after the fire, there were many
rumours.

One was that the alarm hadn't gone off because
of terrorism. Apparently someone had heard a
fireperson say something about terrorism.

As it turned out, rats had chewed through the fire
alarm system's wiring in the basement.

Which, of course, doesn't necessarily rule out
terrorism. I'm sure rats hate us.

And, you know, GROSS.

The other rumour was that this girl Jenna McKenna
(real name) set the fire. Jenna lived on the first
floor with a roommate who was making her nuts.
Katy had promised to try and talk to the housing
department about getting her a new room, but
that wasn't working out very well. Someone said
they heard Jenna say she was going to blow up the
building if she didn't get a good night's sleep (the
roommate snored).

The other other rumour is I guess kind of obvious,
given … Well it's obvious now. Maybe it was obvious
then too.

The other rumour was that Shar set the fire.

Lots and lots of people thought it was Shar.

Except.

Well.

Me.

Although I don't know if I'd say I didn't think Shar set the fire so much as, I guess, for a while I pretty much didn't care.

The morning after the fire I woke up to the sound of hangers wind-chiming as Shar searched through her closet for a sweater. She'd slept on the floor on a pile of pillows and clothes.

"Good morning," I whispered, my throat slightly sore.

"You snore," Shar smirked.

Sun flooded the tiny room, made my skin look white against Shar's red sheets, specimen-like. I closed my eyes for a second. Felt still. Calm.

"Allison! Wake up, let's go. I'm starving."

On the elevator ride Shar grabbed my hand, her touch sending a tiny quake down the steps of my spine. When the doors opened she hooked my pinky in hers and we walked down the hall to the front door where Hope was standing with a bunch of engineering students in matching black parkas.

"Hey! Hope."

The engineers dissipated into the background. "Hey, Allison." Hope threw a quick, uncertain glance at Shar, a fleeting eyeball like you'd give a deadly spider ten feet away.

"I just wanted to say," I stammered, "uh, thank you. I didn't say thank you. Last night. So."

"Oh. Fuck. Any time. Um." Another glance. "Are you okay?"

"Just like a tiny sore throat."

There was a sharp tug on my pinky.

"Okay, well. Take care." Hope waved.

Shar grinned. "Let's get out of here."

For the next few days Shar seemed to be in pretty decent spirits. The day after the fire we skipped school and spent the whole afternoon sneaking from movie theatre to movie theatre watching the beginnings and endings of whatever was playing. We went to the gym to watch the STEP IT UP class and eat doughnuts (leaving the half-empty box in the change room). We bought matching winter boots with silver buckles on them. Shar even started looking up overseas exchange programs with this idea that second year we could get the hell out of town and maybe go someplace far less lame. Maybe Turkey or China. Or France.

Then, less than a week after the fire, Shar got a call to come to security for an interview.

"About what?"

"What do you think?"

She sat in a room with security for an hour. Some puny guy with a pubic moustache and a pukey tie, she said. Shar said the guy was sweating the whole time.

Someone had sent security an email saying they believed Shar was the arsonist responsible for the fire at Dylan Hall. Security said the email was co-signed by two people who lived in Dylan. Shar said she spent the entire interview trying to see through the paper so she could read the names of the bitches who wrote the email.

"Bitches," she spat.

"Could have been ANYONE." I said. "You didn't do it. So don't worry about it."

"Stop calling me paranoid."

"I never said you were paranoid."

The next day, at breakfast, we got into a fight because I said I wanted to go and grab a card for Hope. For saving my life.

The word "life" had an immediate impact on Shar. It

was as though I'd thrown it like a crumpled-up ball of paper that had hit her in the forehead. She tucked her chin into her chest and stabbed at her coffee with her spoon. "I don't think your life was ever actually in any danger, Allison."

"I guess. I wonder if Katy could have died though."

Shar took a slow sip of her coffee, carefully placing her lips on the rim of her chipped red and white coffee cup. Then she said, "I thought it was all smoke."

"Yeah but." A tiny cloud in the sky turned the bright light that had been streaming in through the diner window into a soft, slightly gloomy glow. "It's the smoke that gets you, right?"

I think that's true. Although it seems like a bit of a weird thing to say when you consider how destructive fire is. How is it possible that something as mundane as smoke could be the real killer?

"Okay, Allison, but you were never in any danger of dying." She didn't say it like she normally would have; instead, she was leaning forward with a serious look in her dark eyes. Confrontational.

She seemed … upset. Or not upset. Withdrawn. Like a person sitting deep within themselves or retreating there, leaving their face empty like a sandbox after recess.

"Look. Let's forget it, okay? Let's talk about something else."

When breakfast was over Shar said she was tired and wanted to go back to her room to nap. I walked her back to dorm, and then, because I couldn't think of what else to do, headed to class.

Introduction to Women's Studies. Jefferson Building. A class composed entirely of women, except for, of course, Jonathon, who apparently no longer wore a top hat. I grabbed a chair at the back of the classroom and noticed that everyone had a typed and stapled stack of papers with them.

At the front of the class the professor sat next to a big box she'd labelled "ESSAYS" with a red marker.

Essays? Scrambling through the recycling bin that was my brain, I scanned every memory I had for that phrase. Essay. Essay? I had a vague recollection of a couple stapled sheets of paper sitting under the stack of unopened course packs.

Shit.

The lecture that day was about this woman who said that we needed to stop depending on people in ivory towers to tell us what to do and what to think. The professor (Professor Women's Studies?) made this big show of wandering through the seats as she talked, bangles jangling as she touched people's shoulders, like a kid playing Duck, Duck, Goose, only really serious.

Who is telling us what to think, the professor wanted to know. "Thoughts? Someone? Who is telling us what to think?"

Is it me, I wanted to say, or are professors all really paranoid about what people are thinking and why?

Jonathon raised his hand. "Ah perchance could it be said, ah, that we are all soaking in the irony that you, uh Professor, are in a position to tell us what to think? Or at least have a heavy hand in moulding our thoughts when grading our fledgling papers?"

The class collectively turned to give Jonathon a disdainful glance. Fledgling papers?

What a weirdo.

"Well, yes," Women's Studies replied, raising her wrist so that her bracelets clanged together like wooden spoons in a drawer, "although I think we'd ... I think I'd like to think our job is to guide you, not mould you. We want to make you think, not tell you what to think."

"Of course."

The debate raged on for another forty minutes before class finally let out and I slunk up to the front of the room.

"Excuse me? Um. Professor?"

Up close, I could see Professor Women's Studies had red lipstick on. It matched her long red Women's Studies scarf and red skirt and runny mascara that matched nothing.

"Yes?" she asked, rooting through a giant bag for something obviously very small and/or not in there.

"Um. I was in a fire?" More of a question than a statement. "I think we have a paper due today?"

Is there any way one cancels out the other?

Red lips spread out into a wide O. "At Dylan Hall! Yes, I heard about that. I'm sorry … what's your name?"

"Allison. Allison Lee."

"Are you asking for an extension on the paper that was due because of this recent fire?"

"Yes?"

"I think that's perfectly reasonable. Although I will point out to you that in fairness the paper was assigned weeks ago."

"Uh. Yeah. Okay well. Never m—"

"Oh don't give up so fast." Women's Studies smiled.

"Just send me an email reminding me why you have an extension."

Of course this meant that I'd still have to somehow write the paper. On what I had no idea. I didn't even know who the ivory tower person guiding my thoughts was supposed to be, although I figured I could go home and Google it. Heading into the bustle of inter-class traffic, a multi-celled vibrating creature sporting a variety of smells and sounds, I put my head down and tried not to let my freak-out explode out the front of me.

A hand reached out and grabbed my shoulder.

"Hey!"

Jonathon.

"Hey," I responded weakly.

Under the soft light of day that filtered through the hallway's industrial window, Jonathon's face looked like it was about to peel apart, possibly to reveal a smaller, smoother Jonathon underneath.

Jostled slightly by the crowd, he smiled nervously. "Are you all right? I heard there was a fire. And that you were in said fire."

I concentrated on looking at the collar of his shirt. "It wasn't my fire," I said. "I mean, it didn't really get ME."

"Of course," Jonathon chuckled, "what a concept. I'm fairly certain that no one has the market on fire."

"Right."

"I was just going to suggest," he said, putting his hand out, palm up, "not to take up your time. Only that. I overheard. And. If you require any assistance with your paper I thought. I thought perchance I could be of some service."

My phone buzzed. Three missed calls. One from a campus number. Two from Shar.

"Do you have any notes I could borrow?" I cut in.

Jonathon smiled, raised his hand in kind of a weird giddy wave. "Yes! Yes. Well yes of course you can imagine I have a veritable cornucopia of study aids."

"On you?"

"Ah no. Unfortunately, ha ha, or fortunately, that privilege will require another meeting. I could bring them by your dorm if you like. You're in Dylan Hall, correct?"

"Yeah. Sure. Um. Maybe you can leave them at the desk for me? Or."

Jonathon looked kind of majorly disappointed. "Well, if you're not in."

The swarms of class commuters dissipated, leaving the hallway nearly deserted aside from Jonathon, me, and some kid who appeared to be passed out on one of the benches outside the lecture hall.

"Oh I'm just really busy and my room is all … Maybe you could bring them to my friend's room because that's where I'll be until, you know, until my room is cleaned? Floor six room eight."

"Of course I— That would be …"

"Okay great! Bye." I didn't even wait for him to finish. I dialed Shar as I headed down the hall, almost running.

"Get over here," she snapped. "And bring some food."

I ran into Carly on the stairs between the third and fourth floor at Dylan. As soon as she saw me she pulled me off to the side.

"Holy crap! Where have you been?! I've been calling you for DAYS. Are you okay?" A feather of blonde fell over one eye, leaving her other eye to do the majority of the work of the concerned stare.

"Yeah I'm just. You know. Eating." I shook my paper bag of burgers and fries.

"Where are you staying?"

"Uh, with Shar, for now."

"With Shar."

"Yes."

Carly bit her top lip. "Okay," she sighed. "Will you maybe just text me to let me know how you're doing?"

"Sure."

Digging into her fries, Shar said someone had given her a dirty look when she went to take a shower. Not a dirty look, a suspicious look, she said. A fucked-up look.

"DON'T say it was my imagination, Allison."

"I didn't say anything."

After burgers we rented *The Hours*, which is a movie about three women who are all kind of living this life out of the same book, another missed Cultural Studies screening.

We must have slept through Jonathon's visit later that evening. I found the envelope with my name on it balanced against Shar's door the next day.

Would love to speak to you at some future time if you are able, he'd written on the back.

Inside were all his handwritten notes from class.

Neatly photocopied. Even his notes from his paper were there, clipped separately.

"What's JI?" Shar was sitting cross-legged on the bed as she scanned the stack.

"It's him. JI is 'Jonathon's Insights.'" Mr. Middle English was wearing on me a bit.

"The guy is weird. He's probably wooing you. Trying to get into your pants."

"Maybe." The paper smelled like laundry. Which is not a smell I would have associated with Jonathon. Which is probably a mean thing to think.

"Your kids will have horrible skin. Your kids will be lizard kids. People will sell your kids to the circus or hunt them in the woods for sport. Think, your face, his skin."

"Yuck. Thanks for that image."

"Play your cards right you could probably get him to write you an essay," Shar added, tossing the papers on the floor where they scattered.

JI. See also Identity as Construction. Look up new sources.

JI. Ask in class re significance of use of domestic imagery here.

JI. Relearning but always in new forms. Possible idea for play.

JI. All of this connects back to the first things we learned. Isn't that marvellous?

THIRTEEN

February, fall in love

By February, I was essentially living in Shar's room full time. It was not exactly the most convenient set-up. Most Dylan Hall rooms aren't designed for double occupancy. My room had become a (very expensive) storage closet where I kept all my stuff, like, for example, the notes and books for the classes I wasn't really attending.

I'm not sure if there were any rumours about WHY Shar and I were sharing a room or what was going on IN the room. It wasn't a sex thing. I mean, nothing really happened between us, sex-wise, although I guess I thought there was always the possibility that something might.

A lot of our cohabitation had to do with the fact that, since her visit with security, Shar rarely left her room. The very idea of it stressed her out and made her really angry. We'd almost always have some sort of weird fight when talk switched to the possibility of leaving the room. Shar would get all cold and super pissed whenever I uttered some derivation of "What's wrong" in relation to this topic.

It was kind of crazy making, but then on the rare occasion we did go out, Shar developed this habit of grabbing onto me, leaning on me. All of which made things, not okay, but, I don't know, it made sense somehow.

Shar needed me.

In related news, with the investigation ongoing and unsolved, Katy's parents came from Halifax and moved her into a condo downtown that had this really fancy security system. Katy told people it was because she didn't feel safe at Dylan.

The day before she left, which happened to be the day before Valentine's Day, she came to Shar's room to drop off a present for me—a gift from one survivor to another, she said, handing over a large paper bag. It was a shell, a big white conch shell with a pink, sort of sexually pink-looking, inside. It was heavy and cold to the touch, like marble.

"Wow."

Down the hall, Katy's mother, a frizzy-haired woman dressed in mom jeans and a sweatshirt with a big anchor embroidered on the chest, paced, swinging a set of car keys around her finger.

"Take care of yourself." Katy said.

"Okay. Wow. Sure. Thanks, Katy."

Later, turning the shell over and over in her hands, Shar frowned. "Why are people always giving you stuff these days?" she asked.

"She probably just doesn't want to pack everything," I offered, rolling over on the bed and brushing the pizza-crust crumbs out from under me.

"Or maybe you're shell sisters now?"

I grabbed the shell from her and placed it, pink up, on the desk. "No such thing," I said.

"It looks like a vagina," Shar snickered.

Not surprisingly, Valentine's Day was a big deal at St. Joseph's. In fact, St. Joseph's didn't just celebrate Valentine's DAY but Valentine's WEEK, a whole calendar of events, launching with "couples' romantic dinners" at the various dorm cafeterias, where valentines enjoyed Sloppy Joes served on kaiser rolls cut into heart shapes, Caesar salad on the side.

I cannot imagine why anyone would want to have a romantic dinner in a dorm cafeteria. At one of the other residences, couples got pelted with rolls by renegade (I would imagine single) students.

There was a Valentine's RAVE. Hope went. It was run by the engineering department. Apparently, there was a booth where you could go to make out and get your picture taken making out. They had to shut it down halfway through the night because people were using the booth for purposes other than kissing— with photo evidence to boot. A couple of happy-faced-boy and back-of-girl's head pictures ended up very briefly on the college online social board.

And finally there was the film club's anti-Valentine's ZOMBIE LOVE party for the launch of the musical *To Zombie, with Love.* There was a big green oozing zombie heart on the poster. Carly embroidered a large green heart on the back of her coat and pasted up posters all over campus. The week before the party she and the film people in Dylan Hall all dyed their hair bright green, leaving a wake of green foot and fingerprints, sinks stained Jell-O green, and shower curtains tinted toxic yellow.

I'd caught sight of them all crossing campus from Shar's window, a whole flock of evergreen to minty coloured heads, bright against the snow, loose turf heading to class.

True to form, after a week of decidedly not making special Valentine's Day plans and making fun of the

February, fall in love

people who did, on the day of, out of the blue, Shar decided she wanted to go out. One minute she was sitting on her bed turning Katy's shell over and over in her lap, the next minute she was up and getting dressed.

"We're going out," she said.

"Where?"

"Out."

We headed uptown, ending up at this crazy fancy martini bar. It was all velvet and black leather. All the drinks had fancy names and came with a salad of garnishes. When our Goodfellas arrived, topped with black olives and giant pickle slices, Shar pulled the shell out of her bag and set it on the table next to the orchid centrepiece. Picking up her drink, she sucked the olive off the little plastic sword then reached over and clinked the shell with the side of the glass.

"Cheers, Allison. Here's to YOU taking CARE of yourself."

I paused, my lips on the rim of my glass, and watched Shar as she gulped down her drink and smiled.

"DO it."

"What?"

"Toast the shell! Toast to your good health, Allison!"

My glass hit the side of the shell with a half-hearted clack.

By the time we left the bar, the world was a blur. We zigzagged down the sidewalk and across the street, me following Shar as she charged forward toward a little bridge. When she got to the middle she stopped and steadied herself against the railing. After struggling a bit, she pulled the shell out of her purse again and held it high over her head.

"What are you doing?"

She grinned, held the shell over the side of the bridge and, with little fanfare, opened her hand to let it drop. It hit the road below and shattered into a million porcelain skull-like fragments. There was a squeal in the distance, the sound of truck brakes grinding, rubber skidding against asphalt. We turned and ran, off the bridge and up the street, Shar cackling hysterically. Tomato juice and vodka pumped through my body, crude oil.

Many many blocks later we ground to a halt at the gates outside campus. With one hand leaning on a tree, gasping for breath, a shout jumped out of my throat.

"FUCK, SHAR!"

She grinned, wobbling on the grass as her heels sunk into the now soft turf. "Ha ha!"

"Whatever. That was MINE."

"Oh wah wah! You sad you lost your shell from your BFF?"

"What? No!"

She stepped forward and into me, pushed me against the tree. She planted a kiss on my lips, then another, this one hard, teeth flashing over my bottom lip until they sank down, bit in.

"Mmphf!"

A soft chuckle pushed into my mouth, down my throat. The bark of the tree on the back of my head. Shar's icy hands on my face.

It is apparently possible to feel a million things at once, have them pop up and down in your insides like lottery balls.

Stop. Don't stop. Stop. Don't stop.

When she pulled away she had that familiar look on her face, a look of determination and smug contentment. Black eyes. Pushing off the tree, she backed up, focused on me.

"Let's go, Sonny."

Just north of where we stood, we could hear strains of the Clash. Green light leaked through the doors and windows of the Student Union building.

Zombie party. Grabbing me by the elbow, Shar beelined toward the light like a moth drawn to a green flame.

I didn't want to see Carly. More than anything, at that moment, I didn't want to see Carly or any of the film people with their green turf heads. I especially didn't want to be in the same space with Carly and Shar, Shar and anyone really, but especially Carly and Shar.

"No no no no. Let's go," I whispered, jerking my elbow back like a frightened puppy on a leash.

"What? Why?"

"I don't know. I'm tired and I want to go home now. I'm drunk." I'd managed to pull us to a halt and was now intent on standing my ground. "Plus we have to pay to get in."

It seemed important, at that moment, to focus. I tried very hard to breathe in a level of sobriety from the cold air but it just made my head buzz more.

I didn't see Carly and Danny until they were right behind us, all painted up, arms full of plastic bags loaded with party snacks.

"Hey!" Danny trilled, his face blurred by a mask of white and black and red. "More party-goers! Amazeballs! Are you coming to see our masterpiece? We're doing a midnight screening."

I could feel Carly standing beside me, hear her shifting the bulky bags in her arms. Out of the corner of my eye I could see her minty green face, red lips. "Yeah," she said, kind of quietly.

Shar snickered. "Oh yeah, right, the ZOMBIE movie! Nice face, Superstar."

Danny arched a caked white eyebrow. Carly nudged my shoulder.

"If you want to come in," she said, her voice low, measured, and careful, "you know you're more than welcome. I'd love for you to see the movie. But if tonight's not a good time, I can show it to you later."

"SUPERSTAR!" Shar chuckled. "Why. Are. You. Talking. So. QUIET. LY?"

"You know what, Shar?" Carly snapped. "I'm not actually talking to you at the moment, okay?"

"Okay, Superstar," Shar singsonged. "Don't want to rile up the Oompa-Loompas!"

"WOW," Danny mouthed, and moved closer to Carly, who dropped her bags at her feet.

"Shar. Please don't call me SUPERSTAR."

Shar stepped forward like someone about to throw a punch. Danny and I intervened in unison. I grabbed Shar clumsily by the sleeve of her coat, swinging her toward me.

"DING! DING!" Danny hollered. "HELLO! Round One is OVER. I think it's time for a tension breaker. Better yet, how about we get back to our party and you get back to yours? How about them apples?"

Throwing a sharp glare in my direction, Shar pulled free from my grip and stormed off down the path. Before I could follow, Carly hooked my sleeve.

"I know it's none of my business, okay, but if you need ... I just think you should, you know, like, maybe you could use some space from her?" I couldn't stop staring at the long scar cutting crossways through Carly's face, from her hairline to the nape of her neck. At the top, the wound was oozing yellow gelatin-looking pus.

"Nice wound," I said.

"Allison!"

"Okay, okay, but I gotta go catch up with her right now." I tugged myself loose and headed down the sidewalk where Shar was nowhere to be seen. Alcohol and fear aspirated in my lungs, made my stomach feel the want of a Bugs Bunny garbage pail. I ran and stopped and ran and stopped until I hit the main street.

Across four lanes I thought I saw someone standing by the bank. Maybe Shar. But shorter? I waved but she didn't respond.

"Shar!" I screamed. "Shar?"

The figure looked up. Not Shar. Not Shar?

"Shar? Where are you?"

I remember standing on the curb. My feet were numb and my thighs burned from running. I was dizzy, breathing heavily, when suddenly there was the sound of boots striking pavement, running. I felt a push, a thump between my shoulder blades, and my body flew forward. The world spiralled. My palms, then my head, hit concrete and I heard a squeal of brakes.

FOURTEEN

Accidents (keep) happen(ing)

The car that almost hit me was driven by a woman in her thirties who I guess was (also) having a really fucked-up day. Her front tire stopped about an inch away from my splayed-out hand, which I would later discover was covered in road rash. When I raised my head, only recently cracked against the asphalt like a walnut, I could see the warbly reflection of my bloody upper lip in her bumper, which was splattered in dirt (and almost my brain).

"JESUS CHRIST," the woman screamed as she jumped out of the car, her heels *click, click, clicking* as she ran over. "JESUS CHRIST! JESUS what happened!?! YOU! Do you know this girl?! What happened!? Did she trip?"

From my vantage point I could see the scratches on her high-heeled patent pumps.

I heard Shar's voice, what I thought was Shar's voice, but I couldn't make out the words.

"Hurts." The word spurted out with a cough, a piece of my front tooth, and a horror-movie amount of blood.

Shar's voice, getting closer, zoomed into focus. "My phone's not working! Call an ambulance!"

"Is this your friend?" driver woman screamed, dropping to her knees, beige nylons with little white flowers, and putting her face, very tan, white eye makeup, close to mine. Apparently my face was a source of some concern. She bit her lip.

"CALL AN AMBULANCE!" Shar screeched.

Tell them it's me, I wanted to whisper, but my mouth hurt too much.

Fumbling through her purse, the woman found her phone and dialed frantically.

"JESUS CHRIST! Hello 911? There's been an accident. A girl just fell. On … WHAT STREET IS THIS?"

I went to roll over onto my back but the woman put her hand down on my shoulder, pinning me with two pointy fingers.

"Oh for fuck's sake don't roll over. That's the last thing I need. Lose my job and then fucking paralyze some kid. Yes. We need an ambulance, there's been an accident. No. No, she's not hit. I don't think I hit her. I think. I think she fell. Yes. She's bleeding. Yeah it looks like a lot to me!"

I closed my eyes.

"OH! Hey! Hey! Don't fall asleep okay?! She's losing cons— She's passing out. Hey girl!" She snapped her fingers twice at me, her gold nails flashing in the headlights. "HEY! YOU! Come here and look after your friend. Keep her awake."

There was a pause. Then footsteps as Shar stepped around me. Sat down on the street in front of me. Took my scraped-up hand in hers as I let my face sink to the pavement and waited for the now familiar sound of the ambulance siren.

The result of breaking my fall with my face? Five stitches on the inside of my lip, one on the outside where my tooth actually cut right through to the other side. I had scrapes and bruises on my hands and knees. A scratch on my cheek. My tooth would need to be capped.

I was patched up, told I could go home. I was also told that I was very lucky.

"If you'd been hit by a car instead of just hitting the pavement," the ER nurse tut-tutted, "you'd be dead.

Think about that while I go get you something to
help with the pain."

Shar sat in a little plastic chair by the bed with our
coats in her lap, staring at the floor, periodically
making eye contact then pulling her eyes away. The
curtain that hung around the bed for privacy was
giving everything a soft minty tinge, so her hair
looked kind of elfin. A couple times I almost forgot
she was there she was so quiet. When the doctor
discharged me Shar watched while I got my coat and
shoes on, kind of out of the corner of her eye. Then
we caught a cab back to dorm.

I just sort of autopiloted to her room.

I sat there for a while in silence, perched forward on
her bed, Shar standing over me, still in her coat, her
arms crossed over her chest.

"You should sleep," she said.

She took a few steps toward the door and stopped.

"Are you staying?" I asked, still blurry, reeling.

Steps and voices echoed through the hallway.

"Sure."

I crawled under the sheets and, after a while, she
crawled in behind me. She slept like a porcelain doll,

barely curled up next to me in the bed that was really too small for two.

At one point in the night I felt her touching my back, whispering.

"What did you say?" My voice was scratchy.

"Nothing. Nothing. Go back to sleep."

She was up before I was the next day. Left a Styrofoam cup of coffee and a muffin from the cafeteria next to my bottle of pain meds on the table, with a note.

Take one with food. Gone to class.

I swallowed my pill with cold coffee and just about coughed it back up again when the cold sludge hit the back of my throat. My whole body felt like a crash. Like a mangled wreck that had been left on the side of the road to rot. It took everything I had to pull myself out of bed and into the bathroom, at which point I got a view of my face.

Zombie love.

A face only a zombie could love.

I was standing by the mirror, balancing with my hipbone on the sink while I pulled out my bottom lip to survey my stitches, when Rattles walked in.

"What happened?" she asked. Her voice was still rodent-small.

"Tripped," I said, discovering as I spoke that the stitches on the inside of my lip felt like a bouquet of wriggling ants.

"Tripped?" Leaning over the next sink, Rattles surveyed her own face. Then twisted the taps to turn on the water.

"Off a curb," I added. "Into the street."

Steam collected on Rattles's mirror. She cupped her hands under the water and splashed her face.

"Right," she said into the sink, her skin dripping. "Sure. Tripped."

As she patted her face dry with a little pink towel, I glanced at her wrist, looking for scars. Then I remembered it was a chipped bone. Broken on the inside.

"Yeah, well," I non-responded. "Anyway."

Snapping off the taps, Rattles turned and walked out the door.

By the time I got back to the room there was a message on my phone from the Dean of Students. Jotting down the number on a stray pizza box, I curled up on the bed to dial back.

"Hello, this is the office of the Dean of Students, St. Joseph's College; this is Rita Ambrose speaking. May I have your name and student number?"

"Allison Lee. 9328888."

"Miss Lee." The voice on the other end was vaguely robotic. "The dean would like to see you today. I have an appointment scheduled at three p.m. Do you know where the dean's office is?"

Wow. What if I'd had plans? Or a class. Did I have class? What day was it?

"No?"

"We're in the Pape Building. North end of campus. Walk in the doors and take a right, then two lefts. Office number is 4077."

By the time I pushed through the glass doors of the Pape Building, two hours later, I was covered in sweat, slightly high from the meds, and five minutes late. The secretary, in a navy suit and matching glasses, pointed me toward a row of pink chairs lined up against the wall and told me to wait.

"Can you tell me what this is about?" I asked dozily.

"Sit there please and Dean Portar will be with you shortly."

The Dean of Students, it turned out, was not exactly what you'd imagine a Dean of Students to be. What I imagined at least. I pictured someone like a Hogwarts's instructor: aged, grey-haired, and wise. Dean Portar looked more like a fitness instructor in a suit.

Once I was in her office I sat for a long time in a tiny chair in front of her huge desk, fighting the urge to fall into a drugged coma, while Dean Portar glanced over what I assumed was my file.

Which made me wonder, briefly, exactly how many files of mine there were out there, and whether they all contained roughly the same information; that is, whether all my files pointed to the same conclusion. Like, THIS GIRL IS A FUCK-UP.

All around Portar's office were framed ad-campaign photos for the college, students looking happy in the sunshine, walking together either to or from class, giggling at their new-found social and intellectual lives, I'm sure. In one photo a basketball player in a varsity-type jacket chatted with a kid holding a painter's palette. In another, an Asian girl and a black guy looked to be sharing a book in the library.

As if anyone actually shares a book in the library.

None of the girls in the pictures had stitches. None of the boys had zits.

After a couple minutes Dean Portar picked up a pen and tapped it on the desk. Then she made a small note in the margin. Then looked up and smiled.

"So," she said, her blue eyes taking a long scan of my battered face, "how are you finding your first year at St. Joseph's?"

It seemed a hard question to answer given the state of my appearance. "I'm adjusting," I replied, wincing slightly as my ant lip tickled my bottom front teeth.

"Let's look at your course work."

Let's. Let's do that.

"I've got ... Let's see. Hmmm. Well we have a B and one C. And we've got one, two ... Two passes." *Tap tap* with the pen. Pause. "How would you say things are going this year?"

"Fine."

"Everyone has an adjustment period. Let's take a step away from academics for now." Dean Portar flipped the file shut. "There was an incident. I'm sorry you had to go through that experience."

"Yeah. It's fine." I sounded slightly stoned, I realized, and pulled myself up so that I was at least sitting straight.

"It would be safe to say it's been a turbulent semester so far?"

"I guess. It would be safe."

"Have you been using any of our support systems?" she asked, gesturing with her pen to a stack of familiar neon-bright "ANXIETY" flyers.

"I'm good. Fine. Thanks."

I must have tipped my head up just enough that she suddenly noticed, from her seat, the stitch on my face.

"Oh my goodness. Is that from the fire?" She pointed at my stitches with her tapping pen.

"Uh no. I tripped on the sidewalk coming home yesterday."

Tap tap. My file flipped open. A small note was made in the margin—in red ink.

Possibly something along the lines of "Might not be school problem so much as this girl's own personal date with destruction. Check with lawyers."

"Right. So you've had it seen to."

"Well. Doctors put the stitch in there, so." Not to point out the obvious, but come on.

More tapping. Then another note.

"Fine. Well, Allison, I've brought you in here to update you on the state of our investigation into the fire. You should know that we're addressing the matter as part of a larger issue we're having this year with bullying and harassment."

The phone on her desk rang. The dean paused to look at the display and then continued. "I shouldn't call it an 'issue.' A darker element of school life, possibly. Although to call it something other than an 'issue' does not suggest that we tolerate any form of harassment here at St. Joseph's. I will tell you that we've had a series of incidents we're looking into and that we're taking all of them very seriously. In this case, we do, in fact, have a lead in the matter of the fire, and are following up on it. I know some of the parents of Dylan Hall students were concerned that not enough was being done."

At this point she stopped and leaned forward, head bent down. "If you would like me to contact your parents to discuss the matter I would be more than happy to do so."

"No no." My back broke into a cold sweat just thinking of any conversation between the dean and my father. "No, I've spoken to them."

"Fine. I wanted to have you come in so I could check in on the matter with you in person. Which we have done. I'm going to make a note of that for my files.

Well then. Of course we want our students to feel safe on campus. And I'm part of a larger support system with the goal of maintaining that safety."

She paused again, eye drifting down to my lower lip.

I nodded, neck like rubber. Totally safe. Gotcha.

"I'll give you my card in case there are any other issues or if you'd like to speak to someone in the administration about this matter."

I forgot my hands were all scraped up until I reached forward, leaning out of my chair, to grab the card and my hand popped out of my sleeve like an injured mole. Sitting back in her seat, Dean Portar took a second to give me a look that suggested a mix of concern and what might have been disappointment.

Déjà vu to say the least.

"Right. Well thank you for coming in, Allison."

"Thanks."

I couldn't get out fast enough. I sped past the robot receptionist and pushed my way out the door and into the hallway, where I just about went flying over Jonathon.

Who was sitting on the floor outside the office.

"Hey ... Jonathon!" My first thought was whether

or not he'd want his notes back, or if he'd consider helping me on my next paper.

"Greetings." Tucking his chin into his chest, Jonathon squirmed into a more upright position against the wall.

"Um. Hey. Thanks for the notes. I'm still working on the paper but, um, yeah. Thanks. It was really nice of you to help me."

Silence.

"I'm sorry I didn't get to, uh, see you the day you dropped them off."

"That's quite all right."

"Cool."

Oddly enough, despite my history of basically deflecting Jonathon as much as possible, his bent head and uncharacteristic lack of motor-mouthing were freaking me out a bit.

"Are you okay?" I finally asked.

When he looked up his face was red. Boy tears. Boy tears on a hot pizza face. Jonathon shuddered for a bit, and sucked back a few sobs before answering. "I just do not particularly feel enthused about my visit with the dean, shall we say."

"Oh. Is it about the fire?"

"The fire? No." Unfolding and refolding his legs he fished a tissue out of his pocket and blew hard. "It's a. It is a, shall we say, trivial matter blown into grandiose proportions by a school administration that is terrified of being the subject of some news documentary on campus hazing."

"What does that mean?"

"Can I ask what happened to you?" he said, sniffing back a tear and cocking his head to the side to get a look at my scratched profile.

"Nothing."

"Lovers' quarrel?"

"What?!" I took a step back, unconsciously slipping my hand up to touch the stitch on my lower lip.

"I'm so sorry. Please, don't go. That was a terrible joke. I have a macabre sense of humour at the best of times. I don't suppose you could just pause with me for a second?" Jonathon wiped a tear from his cheek, wincing as his hand grazed over a particularly pimply patch. Catching my stare as I sank to a kneeling position, he smiled. "Would you believe I once had the visage of a newborn babe?"

It was hard to know how to answer that question.

"How about we avoid talking about faces and skin?" I finally suggested.

"A fine idea."

High heels horse clip-clopped up and down the hallway.

"Hey. So. Um. What happened to your hat? Your top hat?"

Jonathon frowned. "It's a urinal for the ruffians of my dorm now, I'm afraid. I erred in leaving it outside my door one day, upended, and a bunch of the boys decided to use it as a repository."

"They PEED in your hat!?" I pictured them all peeing in the hat together, standing in a circle with their pants down, group-ruining Jonathon's chapeau.

"To be honest," he sighed, "it was a welcome change from having them use the door for target practice."

"They PEED on your DOOR!?"

"Hence my visit to the office of Dean Portar. What can I say? Nothing changes. One cannot escape the hells of one's high school past quite so simply."

Just as he said that the door swung open and the receptionist stepped outside.

"Jonathon Innes?"

She tapped her foot a little as we climbed to our feet.

As she scooped him into her office, Jonathon gave me a half-hearted wave.

"Goodbye, Allison."

"Bye."

Outside, the sky was sweatpant grey and the air was wet and cold. Pulling my arms into my hoodie, I headed back to the dorm, my eyes fixed on my sneakers.

Jonathon was right. Nothing changes.

My phone buzzed with a text from Carly.

Need to talk to you NOW. Meet me at Stdnt Union. 4? OK?

FIFTEEN

Jewel

I spent twenty minutes standing in front of the student listings board waiting for Carly.

On that particular day, students at St. Joseph's were partaking of the following:

A volleyball game between the St. Joseph's Grits and the Laurentian College Blazes.

A Christian Fellowship movie night (*The Last Temptation of Christ*) with a cake and non-alcoholic cocktail party to follow.

A vegan potluck thrown by the St. Joseph's Students for the Ethical Treatment of Animals (SSETA).

A concert by the Wild Pluckers in the Jacob Paul Recreational Building (free admission).

Also the Dollar Bills Council (an economics thing, according to their logo) was presenting a lecture on mutual funds in room 423 of the Student Union building, two doors away from where the Student Anxiety Support Group held its weekly meeting.

Students passed in front of the board, checking room numbers, racing off in different directions, with and without books, cell phones, and (semi) matching outfits. Everyone looked busy, happy. It was what you'd picture college to be: full of purpose and activity. At one point Rattles zoomed by, looking as if someone had just told her something really funny. She was holding some tall blond boy's hand, leaning back to yell at someone who was lagging behind.

"We're getting a burger first. Hurry up!"

If she ate fast she could still make her Anxiety meeting, I thought. Although maybe she didn't need it anymore.

As I stared at the board, it occurred to me that I knew as little about any of these groups as I did about what was happening in any of my classes.

Like, we had a volleyball team?

Five minutes later I finally spotted Carly, with her slightly faded green hair, sprinting through the crowd at me like a knight on a white horse (only a little more frazzled).

She was wearing a pair of white painter pants stained green and blue and an old man's overcoat with a bright fuzzy blue sweater underneath. I looked like a prison escapee. Carly looked a bit like an escaped mental patient.

"You didn't leave!" she gasped. "Just. Just gimme a second. Catch my breath. I ran all the way here from the Daily Joe." Locking in on my face, her mouth popped open. "Holy SHIT what happened!?"

"Oh. Nothing. I tripped. On the curb. It's nothing."

A band of future corporate executives breezed past, smelling like cologne and new electronics.

"You tripped off a curb or on a curb?"

"Off."

"Okay." Carly paused, looking through the crowd like a woman on the run. "Okay. Let's get out of here. Let's go to this place I know for coffee. It's, like, five minutes away."

"I can't stay long," I protested, although technically that wasn't true.

A worried look slipped over Carly's face. "Just one coffee, okay? I swear like half an hour TOPS."

The coffee shop was literally a hole in the wall, a concrete bunker tucked under one of the industrial buildings just east of campus. Carly sat down at a little metal table in the far corner of the room and ordered two coffees from the (also green-haired) waitress.

"It's like a green-hair conspiracy," I muttered.

"Oh, that's Dusk. She's in the film club," Carly said.

"Her name is Dusk?"

"Sure. Why not?"

Waiting for Carly to talk, I rubbed my palms, which were insanely itchy, on my jeans.

Dusk came back with the coffees and a shy smile.

"So. Wait. You tripped?" Carly asked, stirring huge squirts of honey into her mug.

"Yeah. Off the curb. It was right after I saw you guys. I just. You know, it was one of those things where you think you have your balance and then—" I let my hand fall to the table, BANG. Spoons, cups, and saucers bounced in unison.

The Goth couple at the table next to us turned to give me a look. It was like getting a mean stare from two angry Shih Tzus in studded collars.

"Sorry," I mouthed.

Carly took a sip of her coffee, placed her palms flat on the table. There was a blast of steam from the coffee machine and then a phone ring that sounded a bit like mine.

"Okay so. Okay. I'm just going to tell you this."

"Okay."

"Just. No agenda. Okay? I know you know I don't like Shar, but this is not about that."

True. Fair. I nodded. My chest did a pre-emptive nervous squeeze.

I had no idea what to expect. I thought maybe she was going to say something about Rattles, whose smiling face was still periodically projected against the back part of my brain.

"Okay. So there's this girl in film club. I wanted you to meet her, actually, before. She's really nice. Her name's Jewel? Maybe you met her. She's super cute? She does yoga with Sarah and Tori?"

The Patties?

I had a vague image. "Maybe." I shrugged.

"Yeah, she thought she might have met you but she wasn't sure. Anyway she's been doing makeup for the film club. She's the most amazing artist. She does the best zombie faces. Anyway." Carly took a deep breath. "After Danny and I saw you and Shar outside last night, she and I were talking about you.

I mean, I was telling her that I'd seen you and that I was worried about you. I mean, with the fire and everything. And with Shar …"

Carly flexed her fingers on the table, then looked up at me for a moment. A strand of green hair fell out of place and she scooped it back into the fold.

"You don't have to be worried about me."

"Anyway. So I was telling her about you. And she was like, 'Shar?' and I was like, 'Yeah, Shar.' And I couldn't remember Shar's last name, which is strange for me, but I described her and Jewel was like, 'I know Shar! I went to school with her.'"

"High school." I picked up my mug and swirled my watery mix of soy and coffee together. The soy looked like it was separating from the coffee a bit, breaking free in shaggy strands.

"Yeah. So I was like, 'Oh.' Right? Like, not like I'm looking for any information. And I'm not, right? But then Jewel said, and remember this is JEWEL, said, 'That girl is crazy. When she was in senior year she was dating this guy and when they broke up she lied and told him she was pregnant.'"

Carly pulled her hands off the table and wrapped them around her coffee mug, her big silver ring clinking against the ceramic. It was only then that I noticed my mug was painted with little devils and hers with little angels. Like the way a kid draws angels and devils, with the same square bodies, four sticks and a circle, a halo and wings versus horns and a pitchfork.

"What do you mean? She pretended she was pregnant? Like a soap opera with a foam belly?"

Carly shook her head. "She TOLD him she was pregnant. Told the whole school. Like, BIG DEAL. HUGE FREAK-OUT. But then he went to her parents, right, because he was freaking out? Jewel said that her parents made Shar get a pregnancy test. Which was negative. Shar told everyone it was a false negative. Then her parents took her to the doctor."

"Shar's dad lives in England," I mumbled.

The café got quiet, all the clinking fading into a soft hum circling around my head, Carly's voice fuzzy like a TV turned up too loud. The ants in my mouth wrestled each other, the soy coffee separating in my intestines.

Carly paused. Looked at me as though decoding my facial features. "Jewel said. Allison? Jewel said that after the whole pregnancy thing, Shar went, like, psycho. Like MEAN psycho. She said Shar was always telling people that her boyfriend hit her. She used to show up with these bruises all over her arms and say that he did it. She used to go to parties and be all over him, then they'd get in these huge fights. Jewel said she'd heard that, over Christmas break, Shar rear-ended this guy's car at the mall."

"What was his name?"

"What?"

"The boyfriend."

Carly frowned. "I could ask her."

"Whatever."

"Hold on a second. Allison. Okay, I don't want to get all, like, after-school-special on you. Okay? But did Shar push you last night? Push you off the curb? Are you sure you tripped?"

"No." My head hurt. "No, she didn't. She didn't push me. Obviously."

Without thinking I chugged down the rest of my coffee, regretting it as soon as the gooey bits of soy began their slip-slide down my throat. Pushing my chair back, I managed a quick "I have to go."

Carly tossed some change on the table and followed me through the scatter of chairs as I struggled to get out of the café before I threw up my coffee. Which I did. In the street. Like, projectile. It looked like it did in the mug. Barfing reminded me I hadn't eaten anything all day.

In my peripheral, as I leaned forward, spitting into the street, I spotted Carly's big black boots.

"Carly"—a line of puke-drool dripped out of the corner of my mouth—"seriously, just leave me alone."

I headed up the street, trying to push my face forward into the wind. I sucked in as much oxygen as my lungs could hold.

"Just." I could feel her jogging behind me. "Allison. Wait up."

"WHAT?!" I spun around. I think she thought I was crying. I wasn't.

"She doesn't have a sister."

"What?"

"Look. If you don't believe me, I can give you Jewel's number."

"I don't want it."

Carly moved forward, maybe to hug me. I put out my hand, kind of accidentally hitting her in the shoulder. She looked mad. Mad and hurt, like her face was about to crack into little pieces. Because of me somehow.

The idea that her feelings were hurt because of me made me inexplicably furious.

"Look. I mean, like, thanks for butting into my life and basically telling me the whole thing is a MESS. But now, just … Just leave me alone, okay?"

Carly's face blurred as I twisted around and started speed-walking up the street, not waiting for a reply, in a hurry to go nowhere.

Back at Dylan people were studying, writing papers, chilling in their rooms. You could hear the clicking of keyboards down the halls, an endless, soft-spoken Morse code, the clicking mixed with various genres of study music. Walking down the hallway, it felt strange to be so close to so many people in such a seemingly relaxed state. A subdued and orderly crowd of floormates.

At some point I'd left my window open and my room was the rough temperature of an icicle or a Korean ice treat. In the dark, I pulled off my clothes and grabbed my robe. Opening and closing my hand was becoming more and more difficult so I just pinched my robe closed, shuffled on my flip-flops, and headed for the shower.

When I was little my parents used to send me to the bathroom for "time outs." My dad thought it was a good room for one to collect one's thoughts, which is kind of gross. Although. It was.

After time outs were long gone, I used to go to the shower to think. Even in residence, I liked the feeling of the tiles, square and hard like tabs of gum. I'd stand in the shower stall, steam collecting around me, and think about stuff.

That night I stood in the shower for an hour thinking about what Carly said. I knew she thought that whatever-her-name's stories might mean that Shar, at the very least, set the fire. But no one knew who set the fire, I told myself.

I closed my eyes and pictured myself standing on the curb, looking for Shar. Did I trip? Yes. No? Yes.

Warm water pounded my back as I raised my palms to my face.

Who was— What was her name? Jewel. Who was Jewel anyway? Maybe Jewel was just like the bitches at my high school. What would they say about me?

Oh there's the girl who lesbo-raped this girl Anne, then tried to set herself on fire.

She said she was Anne's GIRLFRIEND? More like stalker.

Maybe Shar just fucked up with the one boyfriend because of this other boyfriend who beat her up, I thought.

Plus, how would Jewel even know if Shar *had* a sister? Maybe her sister went to some special anorexic school?

When I got out of the shower and back to my room I had a text from Carly.

His name was Rick.

I called Shar. Sat on the bed and waited for her to answer. Nothing.

Called again, waited again. Still nothing.

About an hour later I got my pyjamas on and went downstairs to knock on her door. I was standing there when Rattles came out, all dressed up, glitter in her hair.

"She's not here," Rattles said.

"Oh. Do you know where she went?"

Rattles narrowed her eyes. Shrugged. "She was looking for you."

I waited until Rattles left. Knocked on the door again, just in case Shar was just hiding out.

Nothing.

I called a couple more times after I went back to my room, but sometime around the fifth call I started feeling like a stalker. So I stopped.

SIXTEEN

Scream

The morning after my coffee with Carly, I felt unknitted. I lay in bed for what felt like minutes but was probably hours, staring at the sky through my window. Shar still hadn't called. Other than the Christmas holidays, it was the first time since the beginning of the semester that I'd been out of contact with her for that long.

I got up and walked around the hallway. Carly wasn't in her room (not that I was especially excited about seeing or talking to Carly). A couple students were on their way to class and paused to ask me about my face.

Eventually I went to Women's Studies class, late, if only to see Jonathon. (As an aside, it cracks me up that after years of getting in trouble for being late at high school, in college no one gives a shit about people being late for class. Which makes me wonder what the big deal was.)

Jonathon was MIA, so I slipped back out and decided to head on up to his dorm, because I couldn't really think of anything else to do.

I knew, somehow, that Jonathon lived in Trident Hall, a coed residence that had a rep for being a "party dorm." The top two floors were for engineering students. Fifteen years ago some kid took acid after exams and jumped out a window, plummeting eight floors to his death. Right before he jumped he made himself a pair of tiny wings out of toothpicks and gum. Now Trident was the only dorm where the windows had little grates on them, even though there were engineering students, and crazy students, and gum and toothpicks, in just about every dorm.

There was a crowd of boys playing hacky sack on the pavement outside when I got there.

I watched a couple rounds (of what turned out to be a pretty ridiculous way to pass the time) before butting in. "Um. Do any of you know where Jonathon lives? What his room number is?"

I knew the college had a policy of not giving out information about dorm residents unless the person had a name and a room number.

"WHICH Jonathon," a guy in a lumberjacket and torn-up jeans smirked, side-kicking the hacky sack up and to the left. "Dude, there's like a million Jonathons here."

"Um. I don't remember his last name." I wondered briefly if I looked like the kind of girl who'd be inquiring about Jonathon with some sort of flirty motive and whether or not that would help me get inside.

Another guy, with a huge beard, who was also (more appropriately it seemed to me) wearing a lumberjacket, tipped the hacky up, snatched it out of the air, and said, "Dude, you should give us more info. Is he a black guy?" He tossed the hacky back up, smacking it with the side of his foot. "White guy?" Volley. "Yellow guy?" Volley.

More kids showed up, expanding the circle to camp singalong size.

"Yo! Buddy! Over here!"

Pushing back against the crowd, I struggled to maintain eye contact with the lumberjacks. "He's a white guy? He's kind of a ..."

How to put this? His face is like ...? No. Avoid metaphors.

"He has kind of bad skin?" I finally offered.

I was assuming this detail would only level the field but instead they all burst into hysterics. "The PISSER!" Lumberjacket #1 laughed, missing the hacky sack in the process.

"Dude!" Lumberjacket #2 shook his head and widened his eyes in a less than subtle warning to shut the fuck up. Picking the hacky up off the ground, he leaned toward me and apologetically mumbled, "Dude! Sorry. That Jonathon's in room 502 but he's not home, man. I think he's moving out."

"What?" Where the fuck was everyone going?

Hacky sacking continued. The crowd pushed together, looking not unlike the circles that penguins form in the cold to keep themselves warm.

I turned down the hill. Two steps and I plunged my foot into a cold icy puddle.

"Fuck."

"HEY!" Lumberjack #2 poked my back. "HEY! Do you want us to leave him a message?"

"No."

I was about halfway down the hill when I caught what I could only describe as a tiny chill, a puff of cold air that crawled up the sleeves of my coat and into my chest like a ferret.

Shar?

I only saw her from the back but I knew it was her,
standing on the sidewalk outside the little coffee
shop on the hill between the dorms. She had her
black coat on, the one that wrapped around her body
and tied around the side. When she swivelled slightly
I noticed she was holding a book against her chest.
She had her head cocked to the side, looking up at a
boy. He was tall, with a blue baseball cap covering
what looked like short or non-existent hair, wearing
a bright blue football team (of some sort) jacket and
grey sweatpants.

Sweatpants and sneakers.

He was standing over her like a crooked but
dominant telephone pole. Smiling.

I'd walked up to them before I even realized what
I was doing or had any idea what I would say. I
touched Shar on the shoulder and she spun around.
Smiled wide. The kind of deflective smile used by the
polite as a way of escape.

"Oh. Hey."

"Hey! I've been calling you."

"Yeah," Shar said, throwing another quick smile at
the boy.

"Oh." I stood. Waited for Shar to separate from the boy, to explain where she'd been, why she hadn't answered my calls. She was standing differently, like her whole being had gone through the dryer or been cooked soft.

"I think my phone's on silent," she finally added.

"Okay. So. What are you up to?"

Shar took a step back, bumping into the boy who leaned forward over her shoulder. Smiled again.

"Allison, this is Jeremy. Jer, this is Allison, from Dylan."

"Hey. Nice to meet you." His teeth were picket fences of perfection and his hands were the size of baseball mitts.

"You too," I said, reluctant to stretch out my hand, although I did.

As Jer grabbed and quickly released my paw from his mitt, Shar stared at me and then at the empty space behind me.

Finally Jer straightened, grabbed Shar by the waist, and twirled her toward him into a hug. "Okay, well. I gotta go. But um. You should come to Trident. Fifth floor. You can bring, uh ..." Jer jerked his head in my direction.

"Allison," I repeated.

I turned away and began walking very slowly down the hill. I could hear the soft squeal of the college shuttle bus's brakes on the hill, the scuffing sound of boots on the sidewalk. Eventually Shar came up next to me and then passed me at a brisk pace. I followed.

I didn't want to be the first to say something. The first person to say something in situations like these—awkward situations where one person starts acting differently before the other one does—has the disadvantage. Finally Shar sighed and ground to a halt.

"You're being a bit weird, Allison." Strands of her hair lay across her face like spiderwebs.

I picked the most convenient course for the time being. "What? No I'm not. I was just wondering why you didn't call me back."

"Wow. After seven phone calls?" Shar's voice cracked with sarcasm.

"Yeah." So her phone wasn't on silent.

"Not that you need any of these details, Allison, but I met Jer last night at a diner. You were all MIA so I was eating solo. He just happened to be at Sam's."

"Okay."

"He's helping me with my paper." Shar tipped the book she was carrying so that I could see the bright green lettering: SOCIOLOGY. Green on red, with a picture of a split pomegranate. Since when was Shar taking sociology, I wondered.

"That's great. Why are you saying I'm weirded out? I'm not weirded out."

"Allison." Leaning forward, Shar grabbed and squeezed my elbow. "You look like you just swallowed, like, a fucking tampon or something! Shake it off."

She held me for a second more, then dropped my arm, a little stiffly, and turned back toward the dorm. "I'm going to this party thing, Allison. You can come if you want."

When we got into the elevator she said she needed a nap.

"If you want to come, drop by later and we'll walk over," she suggested, scooting out of the elevator without looking back.

I was at Shar's at eight-fifty p.m. She opened the door and pointed to the bed, where I sat on a pile of what I quickly realized were my clothes while Shar finished up her eyes. A low hum of rock and roll filled the room.

"How's your stitches?" she asked, layering a line of charcoal above her eyelashes.

"They itch," I said, noticing another ball of my stuff shoved into a corner. "The ones on the inside of my lip are already coming loose a little." I bent my lip open in her direction to show her but she didn't seem to notice.

"You know that crazy bitch who almost killed you? When they were loading you into the ambulance she was all over me. Freaking out. Like, a crazy person. She wanted me to give you her number," Shar said, breaking into my daze and sounding suddenly like herself.

"Oh yeah?"

There was another silence. The muffled sound of voices in the hallway, what sounded like shouting.

"I thought maybe she wanted to give you a shell," she chuckled.

"Right," I laughed.

Technically, I was short a shell.

"I gave her a fake number and told her your name was Madison."

Madison. Madison? The named blinked in the corner of my eye, a flashing red light.

Like. Your sister?

"She didn't get my name from the cops?" I finally asked.

"Nope. That woman was borderline. Did you see her? She looked like a tanning salon reject. She looked like a cocktail party reject. I bet she was driving drunk."

"Is that what the cops said? That she was drunk?"

"No. The cops are idiots." Stuffing her makeup back in her bag, Shar flipped off the stereo. "You should come get your stuff and bring it back to your room tomorrow. It's all over the place."

Before we left, as I was sliding on my coat, Shar looked at me through the mirror over her desk and said, "I told you it was never serious with girls, right?"

"Yes."

To be perfectly clear, I KNOW that sentence should have been my warning shot, my signal not to go to the party.

Of course. If you know me by now, you know ...

It wasn't.

The Trident party was not unlike the frat party I'd been to at the beginning of the year. By the time we got there the building was a mechanical heart of pulsating party-goers. Inside, every hallway was lined with bodies—drunk, screaming students roaming in and out of rooms with beers and plastic cups held in increasingly precarious grips. Jer's room, in the corner by the stairwell, was packed with boys and girls in various states of making out and wasted. One girl sat slumped on the floor, her head on her knees, her cup dangling between her thumb and forefinger. Two other giggling girls were hunting through Jer's drawers. Another couple in matching St. Joseph's T-shirts and blue jeans writhed entangled on the bed under a poster of some guy jumping in the air with a basketball. The walls were covered in pictures of people doing various things with basketballs: dunking them, throwing them, bouncing them on the ground. Besides basketball, Jer was clearly a big fan of rap; a full-frontal Auto-Tune assault boomed from the massive black speakers that stood like soldiers at the doorway.

Jer sat on the floor by the stereo, bumping his head to the rhythm.

"LITTLE BUSY IN HERE! SQUAT IT ON THE FLOOR!" he hollered over the noise, pulling Shar toward him.

"JUST NEED TO GET OUR DRINKS!" she hollered back.

"IT'S ALL IN THE BATHROOM. HELP YOURSELF."
Jer shot me a quick look. "HURRY BACK, BABY."

The fifth-floor bathroom had been converted into
a bar, with bags of ice in every sink and bottles of
booze wedged among them like tombstones. In
slightly less bombastic noise conditions, we took two
shots each. Then I grabbed a bottle of gin and poured
what I thought was lime mix in to top it up.

"I thought you weren't into this stuff," I said, taking
a slug from the bottle.

"Drinking?" Shar scoffed.

"No, this." I gestured widely at the space around me.
"Since when are you all 'Let's party'?"

"You know," she replied, grabbing the bottle and
taking a longer swig, "what you don't know, Allison,
is a lot."

"I know."

"You're always TELLING me that you know."

"I know."

"But you DON'T know."

She turned to appraise herself in the mirror,
smoothing down her hair and wiping a tiny smudge
of black off her cheek.

"Stop staring at me, Allison."

A blast of music entered the bathroom on the heels of screaming college girls.

Shar headed back to Jer's room, with me in close pursuit.

I'm not sure how much detail you need about the next few hours. From the time we arrived in Jer's room I just sat on the bed with the wriggling make-out duo and watched Shar flirt with Jer in a way that was completely unlike the person I knew. At some point in the evening Jer pulled out his collection of belt buckles.

"Got the TITTY INSPECTOR BADGE. Sweet. Got. Oh this is the Salami Samurai. Oh YEAH. Check this out. Party in the FRONT! Poker in the … GET IT?!"

The crowd erupted. Wow. Buckles are HILARIOUS. Shar giggled, flapping her hands in front of her face. TOO FUNNY. A foot hit me in the back and I grabbed my drink and stormed out.

After that I wandered in and out of rooms, each one exactly alike, a house salad of teenagers and booze and making out and posters of guys playing sports. Boys grabbed me around the middle, grinded against my leg, grabbed my arms. I struggled free, tumbling like the world was on spin cycle.

By what felt like midnight a couple doors were locked, underwear slung on the handle.

The drill for people like me in situations like these is that we're supposed to leave. That's the unwritten rule. We're supposed to get out of the way. It's not just about being a lesbian, obviously. I'm pretty sure this happens to straight people too. It seems to happen to lesbians a lot though. Because we're such idiots, I think.

Maybe if I wasn't rocking a couple bruises and tasting the stitches in my bottom lip I would have just disappeared. Maybe if I hadn't just spent whatever number of weeks with Shar where we were, like, the only two people at St. Joseph's, I would have disappeared.

Maybe if it weren't for Carly and Madison and Rick.

And Anne.

A little bit of Anne.

That, and the feeling, the growing sensation, that I had been thoroughly betrayed, and thoroughly fooled, into loving someone.

Again.

So yeah, maybe if it weren't for all that, I might have gone home.

But I didn't.

By the time I got back to Jer's room I was like the final episode of a really messy reality TV show. I was both barely standing and insanely pissed off, rage wrapped around my face like a hurricane, making it hard to breathe.

Shar was in Jer's lap, her face in his neck as he talked to someone on the bed. Her face in his neck but her eye trained on me as I stood in the doorway, feet cemented. My right lung collapsed. Thin red flames shot out of the scar on my shoulder. A serpent shook its barbed tail in my mouth.

Shar lifted her head, got up, and walked over to me. All the while pointing like a kid at a crosswalk.

"Go home, Allison. I'm so fucking done with this."

She took another step forward, nudged me out of the doorway and into the hall. The bodies around us paid little to no attention as we bumped past them.

I pushed her back. "You don't want me here?" I slurred. "This little show isn't for me?"

"What are you talking about?"

"Why are you acting like this!?" I was yelling. The music was loud. It felt like camouflage. It probably wasn't.

"I'm not acting like fucking ANYTHING, ALLISON. YOU are acting like a jealous psycho!"

"Are you serious?! You're calling ME jealous?" I was screaming so hard my lips were numb. "Oh my GOD, SHAR!"

"LOOK, Allison. I'm not your GIRLFRIEND! OKAY? You can't GUILT me into fucking you, okay? Just because you're all pitiful and wounded."

"WHAT?! WHAT THE FUCK ARE YOU TALKING ABOUT?!"

Shar crossed her arms over her chest. Looked at me the way the bull looks at the guy in the leotard with the cape, right before charging. Her cheeks were flushed, almost bruise purple.

It spooled out of me. Like a party trick. Like a horror show. "You." I could barely translate my jumbled thoughts into words. "You are a FUCKING LIAR, Shar. You know. You think I don't KNOW? I know. I know FUCKING EVERYTHING."

"WHAT THE FUCK DO YOU KNOW?" Shar's whole face twisted.

"I know you don't have a SISTER."

Silence. A millisecond of calm in the storm.

"I know about RICK. I know you crashed your car

into Rick's car. You LIED and said you were going to have a BABY! I know your dad's not in ENGLAND. I know you're a FUCKING LIAR. I bet no one ever hit you. I bet that's—"

She slapped her hand over my mouth and then pushed me into the wall. Screamed at me, an endless stream of noise coming from the bottom of her lungs, a sound that finally rounded out into a final "FUCK YOU!"

I pushed her away, hard, and managed to stumble into the bathroom, dumping myself into an empty stall. I was crying so hard it felt like a prelude to a stroke, like I was drowning, my lungs filling up with something indescribably heavy and dark. I looked up at the ceiling and tried to press my lips together but it hurt too much. Eventually I stuck the side of my hand in my mouth to muffle my sobs.

I cried until the act of crying itself lost all form and function. Then I just curled up on the toilet and rocked. What felt like hours ticked by. People came in and out of the bathroom without seeming to even notice me. Eventually I slipped out of my stall and put my face in a sink of melting ice and floating empties until it started to feel like a face again.

Only a scattered few were left wandering the halls. They were wasted, human slugs, glassy eyed. I stepped over a passed-out body and walked down the hall to Jer's room. The door was closed. No undies though. I pushed it open with my finger.

Empty.

I stepped inside and closed the door.

SEVENTEEN

Harvest paradise

Maybe I don't feel guilty about what happened in Jer's room that night. Maybe that's why I remember it so precisely.

It was quiet in the room. Just a little noise coming from down the hall, end-of-the-night Led Zeppelin that no one had bothered to turn off.

At first all I could think about was the fact that Shar was gone. That she'd left to go who knows where with Jer. Probably back to her room where she was making out with him on top of a pile of my stuff.

Thinking about that made my chest seize, like my heart was a gravelly hole being scooped out with a fork.

Like, horrible.

I looked down on the floor and noticed one of Jer's shiny sexist belt buckles gleaming up at me. Poker in the back. A metal girl standing with her back end sticking out, smiling a little metallic smile. I crushed her with my foot, the buckle's hinges snapping under the sole of my shoe.

Which felt amazingly good.

Then I locked the door. Then I started looking around. That's when I noticed the candles.

I can pretty much guarantee you that, up until recently, every student at St. Joseph's has, at some time, owned some sort of scented candle. Despite the fact that they are, according to dorm policy, illegal, they're really popular student gifts. Mostly because people think students are stinky and need something to cover the smell of pizza and BO in their rooms.

Jer had two candles, Harvest Paradise and Fresh Linen. They were cheap, the wax lightweight and kind of frilly, the outside wrapper plastic and painted with little spirals and leaves.

Fresh Linen was unused but Harvest Paradise had clearly already been burned.

Which somehow made me even more pissed off. Like this guy is such a dickhead he chooses a cranberry spice over the smell of clean laundry and you want HIM?

Fuck you, Shar.

After burning a few seconds, the Harvest Paradise candle started spewing hot waves of potpourri intensity. Mixed with the odour of cigarettes that already hovered in the air, it smelled like Christmas and cancer.

I laid it on the bed on top of a pile of polyester sports jerseys I'd found on the floor.

Experience, if nothing else, had taught me that synthetics burn fast.

Although not if the candle is sitting safely upright.

Impatient, I tipped the candle onto its side.

Nothing.

Clearly if there was to be an inferno it wasn't going to happen "accidentally."

Finally I reached down and dangled a jersey into the flame. I watched it catch the hem, sliding against the material before taking hold. It burned blue and green, then orange.

Dropping the jersey, I waited until the flames were a few inches high and had begun crawling across the bed, gaining momentum, before I backed out of the room.

I forced myself to walk slowly and calmly down the hall, tiptoeing over another sleeping boy, this one in jeans and an "I'm with Stupid" T-shirt. I felt like I was bursting, like an alien egg splitting into pieces, light pouring from every crack. I pulled the alarm then slipped out into the stairway, down the stairs and, legitimately, out the EMERGENCY EXIT ONLY door.

A fire truck passed me halfway down the hill, siren blaring ... kind of triumphantly I thought.

Maybe it was just really loud.

EIGHTEEN

Reconstructing the crime in question

It was shockingly easy to lie to the cop and campus security guard that arrived at my door sometime around noon the next day. It didn't even feel like a lie, just a remixed version of the beginning and the end of a much longer and more complicated story.

Overall I would say it was, mostly, the truth.

"Sure I was at the party," I said, "but I was drunk. I remember looking for my friend, Shar. I thought maybe she was in this guy Jer's room. But when I got there the door was closed. Then I left."

"Did you see anything strange?" the cop asked.

"Strange like what?" I asked, possibly looking for clarification, looking to be helpful.

"Out of place," the security guard added.

"Um. Well there was a guy sleeping in the hall. But I don't know if that's strange," I explained. "This is college."

They wanted to know what time I left. I said I didn't really know what time I left. I explained that I'd taken the stairs down because when I'm drunk elevators make me feel nauseated, which was maybe why the front-door guy didn't see me leave.

They said the fire damage had been restricted to the room of Jeremy Tivens. It had destroyed a significant portion of his possessions, including an expensive laptop, sports paraphernalia, and other personal items. There was also smoke and water damage to the entire fifth floor.

Jer had already reported that he'd seen Shar and me fighting that night, although he had no idea why we were fighting.

I felt pretty secure that Shar would never say anything about the content and history of that fight to anyone.

I told the cop I couldn't remember why we were fighting.

The cop saw my face and pointed at it with his pen.

"Got yourself some stitches?"

"Yes I do."

"From?"

"Fell off a curb. I was drunk."

"Maybe you want to cool it on the drinking."

"Yeah."

The cop asked me, again, what time I left and I repeated, truthfully, that I really and truly didn't remember what time it was when I left Trident.

"Maybe around one?"

"Could be."

Then they wanted the names of everyone else I saw there, which of course I also didn't know. I said there were a few girls and a few boys.

I'm a crappy witness.

I wondered briefly, as I stood in my room after they'd gone, careful to stay in the spot where the sunbeam hit the floor, if anyone had dusted for fingerprints to see who'd managed to pull the alarm that night. I'd rubbed it with my sleeve afterward, but then I thought maybe they would match the fibres on my sweater, so I threw it away.

The main suspect, which I know because he told me all about his interrogation experience, was

Jonathon. It turned out that Jer was one of the many Trident goons who'd pissed on Jonathon's door and in his hat. Jer was also one of the guys who'd grabbed Jonathon and dragged him back to apologize to the basketball player who tripped over him, and as a result broke his arm, on the second day of school.

Weeks earlier, Jer had explained to Dean Portar that the pissing on Jonathon's door was TOTALLY a mistake; he explained that originally they all thought they were pissing on their buddy Keith's door (next to Jonathon's). Keith was a funny guy who liked pranks and was always playing pranks. So the pissing thing was harmless stuff. Typical freshman stuff. Totally not something meant to make someone feel like they were being bullied. No way.

That's what the dean told Jonathon the day he went to see her, right after I saw him in the hall, crying outside the office. She sat Jonathon down and explained to him that sometimes people make honest mistakes.

The whole thing, she explained, was nothing to get upset about.

Although, obviously, the practice of urinating on a door was unsanitary and no one should be doing that on anyone's door, whether that person was inebriated or not. Jer had promised the dean, in a written letter, that he would absolutely cease and desist this practice.

Jonathon was removed as a suspect in the Trident fire when it was revealed that he was with his parents that night, in a fancy hotel with a doorman who could confirm that no one bearing Jonathon's description had left the building after nine p.m.

That's where he was when I went looking for him, by the way, not "moving out," just at a hotel. His parents, after talking with the dean, had gone to the college to convince him to stay at St. Joseph's. He spent their entire dinner begging to be allowed to go home. I guess his parents convinced him to remain, or just refused to let him leave. They bought him a new laptop and let him stay in their hotel room for just one night of peace and quiet. He slept on the floor.

The fire ended up being a bit of a break for Jonathon. A lot of people from Trident's fifth floor ended up getting moved into new dorms. Jonathon got transferred into McMurtry Hall, composed mostly of music students, many of whom were even weirder looking than he was. Certainly none of them looked like they brushed their hair or washed their face.

I was there the day he moved in, kind of helping him move and kind of bumming even more notes off him (a habit that would continue through the rest of the semester).

Adjusting his papers on his new desk, Jonathon explained that it was a fallacy that engineering students were the hardest working on campus. "There have been studies of music students, actually, because of their immensely high stress levels. It's what you might refer to as an ironically grim reality that these people who are learning music, as it were, uplifting melodies, are also the most driven and the most often driven insane."

"Hopefully none of these people will pee on your door," I noted.

"Yes, I thought of that as well, although I must say that if any of these students were to attempt to, as it were, 'relieve' themselves on my door," Jonathon remarked, "I could certainly take them down, so to speak."

Okay. Yeah. Suffice to say. After a long and bumpy road of awkward interactions, Jonathon was kind of growing on me.

"Well," I said, catching a glance at a sloth-like boy dragging what looked like a trombone case down the hall, "let's hope it doesn't come to that."

The first thing Jonathon did when he moved in was cover all his mirrors with maps, hand-drawn maps of fake places. Fairylands. Kind of weird. Better than basketballs, though. He said he didn't have any need to stare at his current reality and would rather focus on a distant future.

Okay, I wanted to say, but fairyland?

"I want to write science fiction on the side when I'm older," he explained.

Weird.

"Have they found the culprit who set the fire yet?"

I was pretty much sure they were going to nail me for the fire, but a week after the cops came to see me the drunk girl I saw on the floor the night of the party, Sasha, came forward and said she thought Jer had a scented candle burning on his dresser that night, which might have fallen and landed on the bed. Jer admitted he'd had a candle but said he didn't light it that night. But it was there and anyone could have lit it in the course of the evening. It could have easily been tipped over by a stray gust of wind.

Harvest Paradise.

Case (sort of) closed.

The final aftershock of the whole thing, or one of the final aftershocks, was a huge raid conducted by campus security. They didn't call it a raid, obviously. Raids happen in prisons, places where residents are held against their will. At St. Joseph's they called it a "safety inventory check," which most people assumed meant they would be GETTING stuff, not having stuff TAKEN AWAY.

The dorm security guards were instructed to go door to door with a giant plastic garbage bag and everyone was supposed to get rid of any and all incendiaries. No exceptions. The deal was that if you got rid of it that day you wouldn't be asked to pay the fine. Everyone had something. The Patties got in a huge fight with security because it turned out Asian Patty had a little grill in her room as well as the toaster oven, both of which they confiscated. She'd stowed the grill under her bed but they found it anyway.

After you gave up all your stuff, if you looked sketchy or unsure, the security guard brushed stiffly past you and went over your room with laser eyes. He found two extra lighters that I didn't even know I had, or so I said.

They left the bumpy black garbage bags out back afterward, by the dumpsters. That night a whole bunch of homeless people busted into the bags and carted it all away. I'd like to think there were some pretty glorious candlelight ceremonies in alleys across the city that night.

From my bedroom window, I thought I saw some flames burning. It looked kind of nice, religious and a little hopeful.

NINETEEN

Sing out one last time

If Carly was happy when Shar and I stopped being friends, she never said anything about it to me. Which is pretty cool when you think about it; I mean, if anyone had the right to an "I told you so" it was Carly. But she never even asked why Shar and I stopped speaking or hanging out. I'm sure she had a pretty good idea as to the why, though, based on what Jewel said and the rumours about the (two) fires that were still circulating.

A couple days after the Trident fire, when I went to pick her up to go to Cultural Studies, I asked if I could come to the next film club meeting. Carly had a bunch of blue dye in her hair and it had crusted over like a plate of leftover blue spaghetti.

She paused and I had this moment where I thought maybe she was still just a little bit pissed at me because of what happened when we'd gone for coffee. I mean, she'd have every right to be. I'd been super mean to her.

"Or if it's a problem," I blurted, "forget it."

Carly sighed. "No, no! I mean, OF COURSE you can come. I'm sorry. I'm kind of fried today. I'm just, you know, in the middle of some drama ... Uh. Never mind. Yeah. TOTALLY. Come tomorrow, we'll be working out stuff for our next shoot."

"It won't be weird that I haven't been to anything before?"

Carly shook her hair-fused head. All around her room, tacked onto the movie posters I'd seen earlier, were photos of zombies in bright green Technicolor.

"Are those photos from the party?" I asked, pointing.

"Yeah. They're great, right?"

"I need to redecorate," I sighed. It was something I'd meant to say in my head.

"You should. You should totally redecorate," Carly mused. "I mean, seriously, this is college, Allison. It's a time to pick new favourites, to try everything on. You know? Practise a little self-liberation. Some RADICAL EXPERIMENTATION."

This from the girl who showed up at my door the first day looking like a high school cheerleader. I tried to imagine what it must feel like to change the way Carly seemed to have changed. Like, REALLY change.

"Fuck," she trilled, "I gotta get my notes together. Hold on a sec."

One of the pictures was of Carly and a tall girl with long green hair like ivy falling down one side of her face and shoulder. They were standing in front of a huge papier mâché zombie, a roaring creature with a huge head and spindly arms jutting forward. All around them people were frozen in expansive dance moves. The tall girl was wearing white painter pants and a bright pink sweater. In the picture Carly looked happy, resting her head on the girl's shoulder, her arm wrapped around her waist.

"Is that your girlfriend or something?" I asked.

Carly stood and looked at the picture. Then she let out a long sigh. "Sort of. I mean, yeah. That's Lila. But. It's complicated."

I recognized the pants, the same ones Carly was wearing that day in the coffee shop.

"She's got a girlfriend. I mean, and I've got a boyfriend, sort of, too. It's whatever. It's hard. I mean, it kind of always is with me and like, LOVE. I suck at love."

"Maybe everyone sucks at love," I mumbled.

"Maybe."

Leaning in closer to the photo, I spotted a familiar face amongst the other dancing figures, a mop top of curly orange hair, intricate blood-red eye makeup.

"Hey. That's Jewel, right?" I pointed.

"Yeah. That's Jewel," Carly said. "So you do know her?"

"Yeah. I mean, yeah. I think I did meet her. Talking with the Patties. A while ago."

It seemed like ages ago.

"Who are the Patties?" Carly chuckled.

"Never mind."

Staring at the photo, it occurred to me that the day I met Jewel was the day Shar and I had our big fight. Wait. Was that true? Yes. Was it possible that Shar had been so pissed that day because she'd seen me talking to Jewel and the Patties?

Carly put her hand on my back. "We should get going if we're going to make it to class."

Overall I would say that Carly was a pretty awesome friend, like, especially those first few weeks after I stopped talking to Shar. Carly would kind of loosely

shadow me around campus, checking in to make
sure I wasn't all curled up in a ball or anything.

It was strange to be doing stuff without Shar, to
feel the physical absence of Shar. Not that she was
completely GONE. Like, even though she wasn't
actually around me anymore, it still sort of felt like
she was … there. Somehow. I'd feel her. In the
library in the French history section, in the hallway
late at night. Lots of places.

I'd heard she was still seeing that guy Jer, although
I never saw them together. Jonathon said he'd heard
that Shar told Jer we'd had "lesbian sex." I guess
straight guys find that kind of thing really hot.

The last time I spoke to Shar was about a month after
the Trident fire. It was a Thursday night, and I was
heading back to dorm after a film club meeting, where
I'd just been made the official boom operator for the
To Zombie, with Love sequel, *P.S. Zombie Loves You.*

I remember it was one of those damp post-winter
nights where all the street lamps form pools of
reflected light on the pavement. It was cold and wet
and I was walking fast when I spotted Shar ahead of
me, her thin shape a shadow in the near distance,
eight or nine legs ahead.

I probably could have swerved to avoid her. Taken a
longer or a parallel route. Instead I caught up to her
at the intersection, touched her shoulder.

She weaved, bounced from my touch, back and then forward, before looking over at me with lidded eyes. She looked different. Not like a new person or anything, obviously, because it hadn't been that long. Just different. Like a photocopy of the person I used to know. Her makeup was smudged down under her bottom lashes and her hair was a tangle, shaken by a clumsy hand.

Maybe it was just the light.

"You," she said. "Ha! Fire starter."

"No," I said unconvincingly.

"Not that I care, Allison."

"How's your new boyfriend?" My voice evaporated as soon as it left my lips.

"OH. He's fah-bulous, thanks. He was homeless for a while, thanks to you, but he's fabulous now. Doesn't he seem fabulous?"

"I guess. If you like that type."

The light changed. Instead of crossing, Shar teetered over to the building on the corner and leaned back against the wall.

"Sooo how are you?" she hiccupped as she rooted through her pockets. "You know what? Fuck it. Don't answer. I don't care. I hate you."

"I'm sorry, YOU hate ME? What does that mean?"

I watched as Shar slowly, laboriously, pulled a smoke from a crumpled pack. The tips of her fingers were chewed up, wrinkly like old carrots.

"You know," she finally slurred, jamming the pack back in her pocket, "I remember that first time I saw you, all covered in puke. On that hill by the frat house. You looked SOOOOO PATHETIC. And you said you didn't have ANY friends. Remember? And I looked at you and thought, THIS person will be my friend. You know? I just looked at you. And I thought, yes. This person will be there for ME."

"Because I was covered in puke and lonely?"

"No." Shar shook her head violently. "NO, it wasn't even true that you didn't have friends, was it? Y'ad SUPERSTAR. You're lucky I got you anyway. You're lucky and I'm not. Because you're all the same. You all fuck off eventually. So. Fuck you all."

"That's not true." I watched the flame from her lighter dodge around her cigarette, endlessly missing its target. "I didn't do anything! You fucking hooked up with the jock, you told me you don't like girls. I lo— I cared about you and you just LEFT!"

"Oh I see! So you didn't do ANYTHING? HA! Blah blah blah, Allison. Like you never do ANYTHING."

Everything I said she twisted, tore in two, threw back at me. "That's not what I'm saying, Shar!"

"HEY! DON'T act all innocent with me." She looked up, eyes black. "You were getting ready to BETRAY ME. YOU were looking for dirt on me. Hanging out with that bitch JEWEL! Hooking up with that midget cheerleader. Fucking Rattles told me you were all hanging out with her."

"What?" My face got hot. I stepped toward Shar. Her head was back against the wall, her eyes closed. My heart pounded, expanded. Ridiculous. "Shar, that's not what happened. I didn't betray you! I wasn't going to leave. I wasn't going anywhere! That doesn't even make sense!"

I was standing about a foot away, my hand reaching out, almost touching the skin of her wool coat, when her eyes opened.

"Shar, why did you lie?"

"Lie?"

"About ..."

About everything, I wanted to say, not even sure what that meant.

Shar took a long drag, smiled a soft smile.

"You wanna know something? You know what I said

to Rick that night I smashed his fucking ugly Jeep in the parking lot of Hal's Amazing Donuts? I said, 'If you really loved me, you wouldn't have cared. So there was no baby. So what?' And he was like, 'Well. If I did care, I don't care anymore.'" The smile evaporated. "Fucker."

"Shar."

"He broke my heart. He deserved what he got. I gave him what he deserved. And you." Pointing her smouldering cig at me, Shar narrowed her eyes. "You broke my heart too."

"This is what you get to do when your heart is broken?"

"You all deserved what you got. Enjoy your new wounds, Allison. Consider them a fucking parting gift."

And she walked off, up the sidewalk.

"HEY!" I shouted.

She spun around and gave me the finger, and walked away.

It's possible to still be heartbroken and yet happy to see someone go.

I watched her disappear into the haze. Until she was gone.

It occurred to me, standing in the dark, that it was maybe hypocritical for me to ask Shar about why she lied while not admitting that I had lied too.

I had this brief idea that maybe the reason Shar lied, about everything, was maybe not all that different from why I'd lied about Anne, about Anne and me. Because I wanted to be someone else, if only to one person.

It's just a theory.

The only person I ever talked to about Shar was Jonathon. In addition to being kind of funny, when he wasn't nervous and therefore acting weird, Jonathon turned out to be a really good listener.

A couple days after my final shouting match with Shar, Jonathon and I were eating wings in his dorm's (disgusting) rec room and I kind of laid out the whole story. I skipped the part about how I'd set fire to Jer's room, because Jonathon is a bit of a do-gooder at heart, I think, and maybe he's also the sort of person who would turn a (fairly new) friend in to the authorities if he believed she was an arsonist.

"Your friend Shar sounds extremely insecure," Jonathon noted.

"Maybe," I said.

"I'd say she seems sad. And dangerous," he added.

"Yeah."

"Can I ask? Are you over her, do you think?"

"I don't know. It's complicated. I don't want to be her friend. Anymore. But I still feel this urge to talk to her sometimes. Mostly because I'm mad that it's all so messed up. I'm mad that after all that, most of what I know is still just bits of the truth and lies."

"Perhaps that's all you'll ever know."

"That sucks, Jonathon."

"People are strange," he sighed, picking a sliver of meat off his wing and popping it in his mouth. "We are ... Pandora's box. We are ... Bermuda triangles. We are maps to countries that don't exist."

Okay, fairyland man.

Seriously, what a weird guy.

"Is this what you expected college would be like?" I asked, in part to shift the topic away from Shar and in part because I figured he might have some kind of intellectual thing to say about it.

"What exactly are you inquiring about?"

"Exactly what I said."

Outside a herd of anxious woodwind players bustled by.

"Very well. There are a few ways you could look at that question. Is this particular level of school, and further this place, what I thought it would be like as an entity in and of itself? Is it what I thought it would be in comparison to the experience of, say, high school?"

"And?"

"No. Yes and no. I suppose perhaps I hoped along with my fellow students that college would be different from high school, but it's ultimately just the same. Nothing ever just changes. Nothing with people involved anyway. Why would it? Things only change, people only change, with the application of force."

"Is this from Social Problems?"

"A bit of it, yes."

"So you're saying that life will always be like high school unless someone forces us to change?"

"Unless you are that force."

"Jonathon. You exhaust me."

Licking his fingers, Jonathon grinned. "I also think that perhaps we should have something other than wings next time we decide to break from studying to snack."

"Good idea. I don't suppose this pit has any paper towels."

The last story I heard about Shar, which was actually a total overhear from my Women's Studies class, was that Jer and Shar got into a fight at the Tikki Wikki. I heard she pushed a plastic palm tree down and crashed it right onto his table because Jer was sleeping with a couple girls, including Sasha, who was in his room that night the fire was set.

EPILOGUE

Joan of Arc

Thanks to Jonathon, and the fact that, once Shar was gone from my life, I had nothing to do BUT school work, I managed to get most of my shit together for the second half of second term. I mean, technically I was pretty much fucked because I'd missed most of my first classes, first papers, and first tests. But for the last two months I worked my butt off and got EVERYTHING done. Like, every paper. Not that they were genius or anything. I don't think anyone expects a freshman to be genius. I think mostly all they want is for us to show up and … not set ourselves on fire.

I did write what I thought was one intensely kick-ass paper for my Women's Studies class. It was on Joan of Arc, about how different people have interpreted her life: her heroic accomplishments and her death, which may have also been heroic depending on your perspective on these things.

Basically, Joan of Arc was this regular-type French girl who started hearing voices when she was thirteen years old. She figured the voices were God talking to her. She decided to be a virgin, or stay a virgin. Then she decided to save France, or at least help this one guy who she thought was supposed to be the king of France. Then she got screwed over by the system and these people sold her to some English people. Then she was accused of being a witch, and they had a trial, which she lost (of course), and then, finally, they burned her at the stake.

Afterward, as in, after she was burned and dead, she got a retrial and they decided that she wasn't a witch after all. And they made her a martyr instead.

Not that Joan got to rise from the ashes and enjoy her new-found freedom or anything, because she was DEAD.

Part of my paper was about how Joan of Arc is a really great example of a woman who ran against what the expectations were for women back then. There were no other women with Joan on her horse, saving France and generally being a warrior, which is pretty much why she got persecuted and burned up.

Have things really changed? I asked at the end of my paper. *If Joan of Arc were here today, fighting for feminism, would she not be in peril of facing a similar fate?*

When I got my paper back, Ms. Frances (Women's Studies) had drawn a little grey line and a question mark through that part.

Are you saying that feminists today face the possibility of being burned at the stake? she wrote.

I suppose it had been a slight exaggeration.

After, like, forever in the library I also found this book by a guy who said that Joan of Arc might have been a lesbian. He called her a "gender bender" and said she liked to have young women hang out with her. Jonathon said I should take that bit out of my essay because it weakened the flow of my argument and wasn't relevant. I left it in. Jonathon's a genius and all, but he doesn't know everything about Women's Studies. I mean, come on, he's a GUY.

The thing about Joan of Arc is, she wouldn't be a saint today if she hadn't been burned. If she hadn't been set on fire, she'd just be this woman warrior who none of us ever heard of. I bet people wouldn't even believe she existed. But because of the way she died, and the fact that she was innocent and everything, she had a chance to be this inspiring story. She was a regular person, reborn through flames into a legend. Even though I'm sure the actual process was pretty horrifying.

Just so you know, me writing this paper was not about any delusions I have where I think I'm anything like Joan of Arc. Obviously I'm not Joan of Arc. I'm not a warrior. I'm not even a fighter. I wasn't burned at the stake, just burned. Several times.

It's just a paper I wrote about something I thought was really interesting, this story of a tragic fire situation turned into something meaningful and important. I guess it was something I was thinking about a lot as the semester ended and everyone started reminiscing about their first year of college, the things we'd all been through and what it all meant.

The last day of school, the day before load-out, Dylan Hall had this big special dinner in the cafeteria and then they showed this slideshow of pictures people had grabbed off Facebook and Flickr, pictures of residents.

Photos of everyone being friends and hanging out. There was a picture of the Patties doing yoga on the front lawn with a bunch of girls in pastel Lycra. There was a picture of Rattles with other people from the St. Joseph's orchestra. There was a picture of Hope kissing some guy at the Valentine's dance. There was a picture of Katy and two other girls volunteering at a soup kitchen (which someone said they only did once because some girl got lice from the chef hat they lent her). There were a bunch of pictures of Carly: Carly looking like a cheerleader doing the run up the hill during freshman orientation. Carly at the dance with the rest of the *Grease* guys. Carly and the green-haired zombies.

If you looked really closely at a picture of a group of girls sitting on the front steps of Dylan Hall, waiting to go on a canoe trip, you could see a blurry Shar and me in the background, but you'd have to squint.

I remember thinking, when the picture flashed on the screen, that it was probably the only evidence I had left that Shar and I were even friends. One blurry photo.

They called the slideshow "At Play, New Friends."

Which sounded backward to me, but what do I know?

People bawled their eyes out. Mostly I think because they were playing sad songs in the background, like "That's What Friends Are For" and "Closer to Fine" and this ridiculous song about wind and wings.

When it was over, Carly came over to where I was sitting and handed me this Post-it Note with a doodle on it of our two heads. Her head was buzzed short, both on the Post-it and in person.

"Hey thanks. What happened to the blue?"

"Shaved it. Noticed your photo didn't end up in the show so I made you a pic for keeps," she said.

"It's cool. Thanks."

"Okay so! Tell me! What happened when you talked to the dean?"

My academic semester had ended the day before with a meeting with Dean Portar, to check up on my mental state post several accidents and to confirm that my grades were a "satisfactory pass," which is another way of saying "just pass," which is a (metaphorical) warning bell.

Dean Portar talked for a long time about expectations, about how we make decisions about our future. The word "path" came up a lot. She wanted to know if I still felt that St. Joseph's was a good fit for me. Like, for example, given that I was having so much trouble academically, did I think this was where I wanted to continue my academic career as such? Did I feel like I needed a change?

Her face was a serious, solid line. Concrete.

I was like, Gee, way to sell the St. Joseph's College experience. What happened to all those pre-orientation materials I got in the mail telling me St. Joseph's was a place where I could ACHIEVE?

I don't know what happened to me, exactly, sitting in that office, looking at Dean Portar. I just got this surge, this sudden gut feeling, that, this one time, the look I was getting, that look of what could be interpreted as disappointment, was … premature. Or, at the least, not completely right.

I explained that, yes, in a lot of ways it was a crappy year, but, I said, I was kind of trying not to blame it on the place where I was or any of that other stuff. Plus, I noted, I did have this one class, the Women's Studies course, which I did really well in and I was kind of thinking maybe I would take more classes like that next year.

"More classes like what?"

"You know, classes where people question why people think what they think. Stuff like that?"

"Philosophy?"

"Maybe."

Dean Portar took a moment to look at me, kind of hard.

"You seem to be a capable young woman," she finally said, fingering the pile of academic program brochures on her desk. "You've got the world ahead of you. I hope, Ms. Lee, that you'll consider what you want your future to look like and that you'll take steps to make that future a reality."

"I know. I know maybe it's weird," I said, "but I really do think that the step I need to take is to stay."

So. Cheesy.

"Well, Ms. Lee. I'd love to see that happen."

She was kind of … smiling at me.

It was nice to hear someone talk about the future I
had ahead of me without the look of intense concern.
Even if it was just a fleeting grin, I took it as a
positive omen.

"Uh. See you next year, I guess."

"Less in this office, Ms. Lee, I hope."

The day I left Dylan Hall, after I'd done a final sweep
of my room, I touched the mirrors, my desk, the
little holes in the walls. I realized that if I leaned
into the wall by my bed, I could still smell a faint
whiff of smoke. The bottom of the door was warped
and frayed, like an old shower curtain, from water
damage.

It was weird to imagine the slightly less battered me
standing in the slightly less battered room less than
a year earlier, hugging my boxes and feeling afraid. I
felt, like, a million years older than that girl.

I left my key on the bed. I was going to leave Jennifer
Taylor's ID behind, but then at the last minute I
figured I might need it next year, so that was the one
thing I kept. And then I closed the door behind me.

I resisted the urge to trace the letters etched into
the glass case of the new fire extinguisher, "BREAK
GLASS IN CASE OF FIRE," while I waited to take the
elevator to the main floor where my dad was waiting,
anxious to depart and avoid traffic.

After a summer working for my dad (I know! What
thrills!), I'll be back at St. Joseph's next year and,
kind of, starting all over again. Jonathon asked
me if I wanted to live with him and this other girl,
Lucy, who's a cellist in second year. Lucy already
has a house and it's really nice. Back garden
and everything. I said yes. I mean, I don't know
if Jonathon and I will be the most compatible
roommates because sometimes when he talks I have
this insane urge to roll my eyes. But he's a good
student. And, as far as I can tell, he's not crazy in
any way that might cause me (further) physical
damage.

And, you know, he's been a really good listener and
he's basically the reason I passed my courses. Now
that he's out of Trident his skin even looks a little
better.

Just a little, but that's pretty good.

Carly is living with a bunch of girls from film club
next year, including Lila. I don't think it's the best
idea, but who knows. Carly said I should make
sure there's a couch in my place so she can come

and crash if there's drama. Which is a distinct possibility.

I pretty much owe her LOTS so. Yeah. I'll make sure there's a couch.

I don't know where Shar is going next year. I don't think she'll be coming back to St. Joseph's. I could be cynical and imagine that she'll go to some other college, get her clutches into someone new, a girl she'll become best friends with, and that girl will think Shar is like this amazing BFF or even a new beginning. When really it'll all just be the same thing, the beginning of another cycle of manipulation and lies and destruction.

I don't want to think that, though. I want to think that maybe she'll figure out some way to stop lying, to stop hating the people she loves and causing disasters.

Maybe that's me saying I think she loved me. I don't really know if that's true.

I guess the bottom line is that I want to think Shar can change.

I want to think it's possible for both of us to fall in love (with different people, mind you) and have it not be the sort of thing that leaves any lasting tissue damage.

Which is me saying I want to think that I can change too.

I know I'm not a hero, or a mythical creature. But I can't help thinking that as a person with a vast (vaster than most) amount of experience with fire and love, with general incendiariness, and as a person who has survived more than her fair dealings with fire, I could end up being one of those creatures that can emerge from the flames ... better. Or, at the very least, I can be one of those people whose story about fire and love (of country or girl) is an inspiration.

Not now, of course. I mean, no, this story is probably not all that inspiring.

But, someday, it could be. Someday I could do something, be something, inspiring.

Hey.

You never know.

Acknowledgments

This book had many audiences and editors. It was read, in various stages of development, in front of willing (or seemingly willing) crowds at various writers' festivals, and so I am grateful to the organizers of the Ottawa Writers' Festival, Kingston Writers' Festival, Vancouver Writers' Festival, and Toronto's Pride Literary Stage (to name a few). To the students of the various classes who sat through readings and gave feedback: thank you. Also thank you to my literary agents Sam Hiyate and Alison McDonald of The Rights Factory for emotional and editorial support. To Susan Rich for her keen insights in the early stages. To my editor Lynne Missen for all her amazing work bringing the manuscript around the final lap. To the Ontario Arts Council and the Writers Reserve grant participants, thank you for the cash that made taking the time to write this possible. And finally I should thank my parents, who paid for me to go to McGill University, where the seeds of this story were sown, while I was not going to class.